What the critics are saying:

On *Inside Lady Miranda*

The Best Reviews… "Ms. Kelly does a superb job of bringing sensual excitement with a touch of humor into this story. It will make your toes curl, have you breathing hard and desperate for more. It is erotica at it's best… " - *Tracey West*

On *Miss Beatrice's Bottom*

Timeless Tales… "**Miss Beatrice's Bottom** is a delightfully fast-paced short story that manages to show the depth of Harry and Beatrice's feelings for each other in a few short pages…the love affair between the two main characters is hot and sizzling, but full of love and affection and doesn't leave the reader feeling empty." *-Brenda Gill*

On *Lying with Louisa*

The Romance Studio… "Ms. Kelly pens a wonderfully written story filled with marvelous chemistry and emotion. **Lying with Louisa** is an extremely steamy tale that packs quite a punch in a few pages…This tale is a sensual delight that I highly recommend." *Larenda Twigg, The Romance Studio*

On *Pleasuring Miss Poppy*

TALES OF THE BEAU MONDE
An Ellora's Cave Publication, July 2004

Ellora's Cave Publishing, Inc.
PO Box 787
Hudson, OH 44236-0787

ISBN #1-4199-5000-2

Edited by Briana St. James.
Cover art by Syneca

TALES OF THE BEAU MONDE

Inside Lady Miranda

Miss Beatrice's Bottom

Lying With Louisa

Pleasuring Miss Poppy

by Sahara Kelly

INSIDE LADY MIRANDA

Chapter 1

Looking at her reflection in the tall mirror, Miranda Montvale realized that this scheme was complete and utter madness.

The neckline of her dress was definitely too low. She tugged, but nothing would make it rise more than a fraction of an inch and she was desperately afraid that if she sneezed her nipples would make their debut.

It had to be one of the worst ideas she'd ever had. She turned to the woman seated behind her.

"Are you sure about this dress, Letty?"

Letitia Randolph stood and stretched, pushing her hand to her lower back to ease the ache.

"I mean, being *enceinte*, you might be prey to some odd fancies, you know..."

"Miranda, this is *not* an odd fancy. Nor is it actually *my* idea. *Nor* do I get 'odd fancies'. I am expecting a child, not insane. Although I must admit there have been times when I've wondered if they were one and the same..." she sighed and eased her bulky body back onto the chair.

Miranda turned back to the looking glass. "Well, it still looks indecent," she complained, twisting this way and that to see her reflection.

Letty sighed. "It's supposed to look indecent. How are you going to catch Nicholas Barbour's attention, let alone seduce him into bed, if you don't look indecent?"

Miranda bit her lip.

"Look, 'Randa, if you don't want to go through with this, I've told you that John and I will raise the money for you somehow…"

Miranda immediately shook her head, sending fiery curls shimmering around her neck and shoulders.

"You and John are the closest thing to family I have. You have your own responsibilities and problems, and I'll not be the one to add to them. This plan will work. I know it…"

"I hope you're right. I still think that attempting to win 'The Barb's' bet is a dangerous and silly plan. But I understand." Letty looked down and smoothed her hand over her belly. "In fact, I have to confess that if it hadn't been for John, well…I might have thought about…just thought about, you understand…"

Miranda turned laughing eyes on her friend.

"You mean you'd have joined the eager throng of women determined to satisfy Nicholas Barbour?"

"Well, he is rather delicious-looking, all that hard muscle under those exquisitely cut jackets, and his thighs…Mmm."

"Letty!" admonished Miranda. "You're a married woman!"

"Yes, I know," grinned Letty. "That's a rather obvious fact right now," she glanced down at the next generation of Randolphs. "And I'd never consider doing anything at all with anyone other than John, but let's be honest, Nick Barbour is one glorious specimen of manhood." She licked her lips.

"A specimen who, apparently, is unable to reach his own satisfaction." Miranda gazed at her reflection.

"So 'tis said. Have you seen him?"

A brief impression of midnight blue eyes, wind tossed hair and an arrogant air flashed through Miranda's mind. "Only once—while riding. He galloped past at a furious pace. And oh my, he did have very strong thighs…" She blushed.

"That's not the only thing that is supposed to be strong. You know why they call him 'the Barb'?"

"Because of his similarity to a Barbarian, I would suppose," answered Miranda, tucking a wayward curl into its correct position.

"Oh no," chuckled Letty. "It's because his—um— equipment is rather like a horse's. You know, that famous Arabian stallion...The Barb?"

Miranda turned wide eyes on Letty. "Really?"

"Really!" This time it was a definite giggle. "Of course, having been married, you'll not be shocked, right?"

Miranda snorted inelegantly.

Letty bit her lip, annoyed at herself for reminding her dearest friend of the disastrous marriage from which the death of her husband had liberated her.

"Marriage meant little in the way of physical activities for me, Letty. We've discussed that before."

"Yes, I know, and the fact that Lord Montvale was old enough to be your grandfather certainly didn't help."

"And you don't understand how he could only have...have taken me once. It's the truth. After that first time he never touched me. He'd just—look."

Miranda blushed still at the memories of standing nude before her elderly husband in a pose of his choice, being examined by him and his trusty eyeglass. Even though he hadn't laid a hand on her, there was something infinitely more uncomfortable about being examined while naked than being *held* while naked.

"Well, it's distinctly odd. And it did nothing to prepare you for Nick Barbour, that's definite," nodded Letty.

"It sounds as though there is little that would prepare anyone for Nick Barbour," said Miranda ruefully. "If there wasn't the matter of ten thousand pounds riding on this silly bet, do you think I'd go within two miles of that man?"

Letitia gazed at her friend, standing tall and proud like an Amazon warrior in black velvet. Privately she considered

Miranda an excellent match for Nick Barbour, but knew she'd never be able to voice the opinion out loud.

Carefully, she considered her next words. "Lord Nicholas Barbour has offered ten thousand pounds to the woman who can satisfy him *while he is within her body.* That should tell you something right there. They say he's very big, Miranda. So big that none of his mistresses thus far have been able to take him to the point of release inside their bodies. Do you understand?"

"Oh yes, I understand very well…" A small smile curved Miranda's full lips.

"And?"

"Let me worry about that, Letty. For ten thousand pounds, I can be the best henhouse for the biggest cock to roost in."

Letitia gasped and then burst out laughing.

"If anyone can, you can, Miranda dearest. Especially in that gown…"

Both women turned to the glass as Miranda fastened the black velvet mask over the top half of her face.

The gown was sensational against the white of her rounded breasts and the violent red of her hair. Miranda's eyes glittered through the slits in the velvet mask, and she giggled as she raised her hem slightly and showed off her shockingly black stockings, held up by black ribbon garters. A tiny red satin rose in the center of each garter was the only color she had allowed.

She stood tall, towering over her pregnant friend by almost a foot. Letty knew that if Miranda had not been married so young to Lord Montvale and whisked off to the wilds of Yorkshire, she would have been termed "Goddess" of the Ton within weeks of making her debut.

"Do you have your invitation?" she asked nervously.

"Yes."

"And your carriage?"

"The crest has been covered, the driver is a hire for the evening, and I have taken every precaution, Letty. Stop fussing."

"How can I *not* fuss? You have almost no experience with men, yet you have managed to procure an invitation—heaven knows how—to the home of one of the most licentious men in England. There, you intend to seduce him into bed, and get him to scream out his pleasure while he's buried to the hilt inside you, thus winning you ten thousand pounds. Which you will then take home to Yorkshire with you and use to secure Montvale House in your name. Did I mention everything?"

"Yes."

"There is something very, very wrong with this plan."

Miranda widened her green eyes and stared innocently through the mask at her friend.

"Wrong? How can anything be wrong?"

"Well, what you're thinking about doing—it's not—you shouldn't—you are..."

"I'm a widow who is going to be homeless soon if I don't get money quickly." Miranda reached for her cloak. "I won't be a burden on my friends, and this is as good a way as any to solve my problems, don't you think?"

She took one last glance into the mirror then turned away and straightened her shoulders. A small smile curved around her generous lips.

"You're looking forward to it, aren't you?" asked Letty in disbelief. "You're actually excited by the idea of seducing one of the biggest rakes in the country, and I'm not just talking about his reputation."

"You said it yourself, Letty dear. Nick Barbour is quite a man. I cannot, in all fairness, say I am adverse to the idea of— shall we say—trying him on for size?"

Letty sputtered and threw her hands in the air.

"You'd better tell me every single detail. Take notes—no, better yet, take measurements!"

The laughter of both women rolled through the entrance hall as they neared the door where Miranda's carriage was waiting.

Letty reached for her friend and gave her a quick, awkward hug.

"Be careful, Miranda. This man is no-one's toy…"

"Perhaps he'll be mine by the time this night is over. One never knows. Don't worry, Letty, I'll be fine."

Miranda grinned conspiratorially, and leaned over to drop a light kiss on her friend's cheek. She turned and left the house as Letty stood frowning in the middle of the foyer.

* * * * *

Lord Nicholas Barbour gazed around his small salon with a mixture of satisfaction and boredom.

The select group of friends that had met there this evening had dined well, drunk even better, and were now disporting themselves in various stages of nakedness around the room.

The Right Honorable Chuffy Faversham was stark naked, pounding his cock into Madame Margrèthe LeFond, she of the bounteous tits, and it was *not* the most decadent sight in the world. Chuffy belonged to the school of thought that said nakedness was only appropriate under cover of night. Consequently, his buttocks were whiter than snow, gleaming in the candlelight, and resembling two trembling mountains of custard as they continued their inexhaustible thrusting. He probably ought to think about losing a few pounds instead of polishing off the tray of sweetmeats along with his after-dinner brandy and cigar.

Sir Michael Devonshire, on the other hand, was as skinny as a rake, and completely without hips. Because of this fact, pointed out with great hilarity by his friends on many similar occasions, his trousers would drop to the floor as soon as their ties were loosened. 'Puddle-breeches' Devonshire was living up to his name this evening, because his trousers were in their usual position, lying puddled around his ankles as he stood in front of the windows.

Fortunately, the outside world was spared a glimpse of Puddle's genitals, because they were currently buried inside the woman he had sandwiched between the glass and his slender body. He too was enjoying some continental cunt—Mademoiselle Georgienne Étrange (of the Calais Étranges) was the happy recipient of his attentions. At least if her moans of pleasure were any guide.

Harry Boyd, the oldest of the group, had elected to fuck the home flag that night, and his whiskey brown eyes were closed with pleasure as he enjoyed the attentions of the very British Mrs. Clementine Fotheringay and the frightfully English Lady Jane March.

Mrs. Fotheringay apparently had a talented tongue, if Harry's grunts were an indication of her skill, muttered as they were around one of Lady Jane's breasts, which he was sucking vigorously at the time. His breeches were folded neatly on a side chair—leave it to Harry to be tidy about everything, even his debauches!

Nick sighed. Just another night at Barbour's Folly. It seemed that tonight his home was very appropriately named.

He stretched his arms out to either side and spread his legs widely, giving Annabelle Jordan even more room to work his cock. His shirt was splayed open, just brushing the tops of his thighs, and the rest of his clothes were God-knows-where.

Annabelle couldn't wait to get her hands on him. She'd run dancing fingers up his thighs and over his bulging crotch during dinner, and it had taken him mere moments to free her tits from her dress. That dress had gone the way of his clothes, and she knelt in complete nakedness before him hungrily slurping her way over his hard cock. His buttocks shifted slightly as she nibbled beneath the head.

He sighed again. That damn cock of his was really going to get him into trouble one of these days.

He reached down and gave an encouraging tweak to one of Annabelle's extraordinary nipples—he'd never seen a pair elongated quite like that, and didn't know if he actually liked them or not.

She glanced up over a mouthful of flesh and gave him a grin as best she could.

She was a good sort, really. Nick knew if it hadn't been for that stupid bet she'd probably have taken Chuffy upstairs and fucked him blind for the rest of the night. But that damnable bet...

For the umpteenth time, Nick Barbour cursed his father, his club and his predilection for brandy. For going on six years now, he'd been paying the price for all of them!

It had seemed like a great joke at the time, four bosky young men wagering on who would come first and fill the whores they'd hired chock full of aristocratic semen. When Nick had outlasted everyone, the idea had become firmly lodged in the drunken minds of his companions—Nick Barbour never came inside a woman. When he'd pulled out and the others had seen the size of his still erect, glistening cock, the legend had begun, aided in every respect by his father, the old sod, whose pride in having a son with a lurid sexual reputation was immense.

Nick knew he was somewhat bigger than normal, if there was such a thing, but he also knew it made no difference. What had made the difference was seeing his father drunkenly lurch from woman to woman and from whore to whore, regardless of the fact that Nick's mother was ill at home. Dying, as it turned out.

That night marked the end of Lord Nicholas Barbour's adventures with brandy, although few of his friends knew that nothing stronger than wine had passed his lips in the last six years. When his father had been killed while trying to drunkenly fuck a whore and drive a phaeton at the same time, Nick shrugged and assumed the title. His mother was gone, he was wealthy, young and alone, and content to have it that way.

He also had any pussy he wanted, and once word of the entry in the Betting Book at White's got out, women lined up to try their luck at getting a load of Lordly come, and ten thousand pounds for their trouble.

"Lord Nicholas Barbour hereby makes it known that the sum of ten thousand pounds will be placed on deposit at Coutt's Bank, to be distributed to the woman who shall cause said Lord Barbour to achieve a paroxysm of pleasure whilst within her body. Proof shall be the signed affidavit of both parties, witnessed by a third of their choice.

Pledged this day, fourteenth November, 1813, attested to by..."

He'd signed the damn thing, too. So had Harry Boyd. The die had been cast six years ago, and although he'd come in many different ways with many different women, he'd not climaxed inside a single one since that day. His control was now much discussed, and his cock ranked high as one of the more interesting topics behind the fans of the Ton's salons.

And he was getting bloody sick of the whole damn business.

Annabelle was working herself into a frenzy between his legs, and he was rather amused to realize his mind had drifted while she was sucking him so energetically. He leaned down and grabbed her pussy, working her clit with his thumb and shoving two fingers into her dripping cunt.

She gasped and cried out, dropping his cock from her mouth as she came with ferocious spasms.

"Oh God, Nick..." she squawked, collapsing on the Aubusson carpet at his feet. "Oh my God..."

"You're a lovely lady, Annabelle. My thanks for your pleasure."

He stood, drew his shirt together across his chest, and left the room. It was midnight, the time when Nick Barbour always retired from the festivities.

Watching him was a pair of thoughtful eyes. Sir Harry Boyd glanced at the ormolu clock on the mantel and noted the time. A little grin curved the sensual lips that were still suckling Lady Jane's nipples, although now Mrs. Fotheringay was straddling him and bouncing on his cock like a rider learning to post to the trot. Perhaps tonight would be Nick's night. Harry hoped so. He'd gone to a lot of trouble to set the stage...

Chapter 2

The journey to Barbour's Folly would take Miranda nearly an hour, so she settled back into the cushions and let the rocking motion of the carriage soothe her nerves.

This was her last chance to save her home. The polite letters from the Montvale lawyers had been worded delicately, but the message was the same. Her late husband's estate was in debt, there was no entail or heir, and if she could not provide the sum of eight thousand two hundred and forty-seven pounds to her creditors, she was going to have to sell. What few assets there were had already been mortgaged, and the small amount of jewelry had been pawned and replaced with glass by some long-forgotten Montvale. It seemed that financial irresponsibility ran through that family like the flux!

She thanked the Lord for sending her Louisa.

It had been about five weeks after Lord Montvale's death that Miranda had noticed the odd alignment of shelves in her late husband's study, and had gone exploring. She'd discovered a small hidden passage leading to a room full of—well, at first she'd had no idea what it was full of!

But then Louisa had entered through a different door, and had noticed Miranda's wide-eyed curiosity.

Louisa Cellini ran the Montvale household and had worked there since her parents had left her in the village nearly twenty-five years before. Italian by birth, she had spoken very little English, and when she suffered a miscarriage within hours of being deserted by her family, the Montvales had taken her into their home. She had gladly welcomed the chance to become a servant—first learning a maid's duties, and eventually rising through the ranks to become housekeeper. That she might have been much more to the late Lord Montvale was an ill-kept secret, but Miranda liked her and the two women co-existed as friends.

It had been Louisa who had begun to teach her about the things that Lord Montvale had secreted in his private hideaway.

At first they had just looked and touched, Louisa monitoring Miranda's reaction to what she saw and heard. There were strangely shaped tools covered with the softest leather, shining from years of oiling. There were some wooden ones, and some made of glass, finely detailed and cold to Miranda's curious fingers.

On one wall there was a selection of whips and floggers. The leathers were stained with years of use. One had sharp metal studs at the points of each lash, while another had small velvet roses stitched carefully to the leather straps.

There was a desk containing many well-thumbed novels, which would *never* have been found at Hatchard's Lending Library. Miranda, whose love of learning had long ago outpaced her governesses, had started with a book by John Cleland. "Memoirs of a Woman of Pleasure" had shocked, startled and titillated Miranda's mind, and she found herself devouring the adventures of Mistress Fanny Hill.

As she read, she realized how lacking her own sexual education had been. She yearned to experience what Fanny described as *"lambent fire"* and to be plunged into a *"tumult that robb'd her of all liberty of thought..."*

Her eyes had turned to the strange assortment of tools displayed with pride and she blushed as she realized she was surveying a magnificent collection of *dilettos* as Louisa called them. A much nicer word, thought Miranda, than dildoes.

Louisa had returned that day just as Miranda had plucked up enough courage to widen her legs and experiment! Smiling, Louisa had immediately stripped them both, stoked up the fire in the hearth, and proceeded to stoke up a sexual furnace within Miranda.

From then on, their daily dalliance within their secret chamber was orchestrated by sighs, moans, laughter and giggles, and Miranda learned what her body could achieve under the hands of an expert lover.

And Louisa was certainly *that*. She enjoyed making love, she told Miranda. Whether it was with a man, a woman, a tool or her own hands, she took great pleasure in the act itself and believed that to orgasm each day was to keep one's body healthy and one's mind active.

She was walking proof of her own pudding! Although past forty, her skin was clear and fresh, and even if a few lines were now appearing around her eyes to mark the passage of time, her body remained firm and trim. Her breasts were small, yet full, and her mound was covered with a luxuriant growth of jet-black curls. She loved her body, was comfortable with her own nudity, and liked nothing better than to touch herself with her hands, the toys and anything else she could think of. The word "uninhibited" could well have been defined by a painting of Louisa in the throes of her pleasure.

Any embarrassment Miranda felt had quickly worn off as the two women shared some very interesting sexual experiences. The dildoes had received quite a bit of attention, although Louisa did little but complain about them.

"They do not feel right, Miranda, little one..." said Louisa one day, sprawling on the carpet with legs widespread. She pulled her dildo-of-choice out from her cunt and waved it in the air. "The man is so much more warm, so much more hard..."

Miranda giggled. She had just masturbated herself to an amazing orgasm using her favorite glass dildo and was lying bonelessly across a well-stuffed chaise. "How can a man be harder than wood, Louisa? You are teasing me, aren't you?"

"But no, child. A man is different than wood, than leather, than glass. He is smooth and yet hard, like velvet over iron, and each has many different ridges and shapes to him. And of course he plays with the body first, to ready the cunny for his loving," she sighed and re-inserted her dildo, gently caressing her clit with her other hand.

Miranda felt herself get wet again as she watched Louisa writhe on the floor. Miranda's nipples pebbled along with Louisa's, and she followed her instinct and knelt down beside her friend. Pushing Louisa's hand away, Miranda slid her own fingers towards Louisa's mound, while her other hand tweaked and rolled and pulled Louisa's by now solidly ruched nipples. She lowered her head and sucked on one, making Louisa moan with pleasure.

It tasted flowery and felt strange between her lips, like a small overripe cherry. It was not an unpleasant sensation, however, and Louisa certainly seemed to be enjoying it. Her moans and sighs were increasing, and her buttocks were now thrusting her mound into Miranda's hand.

Carefully, tentatively, Miranda allowed her fingers to probe the swollen and hot tissues, seeking Louisa's clit. There—there it was! One light flick and gasps came from Louisa's mouth, her head rolling frantically from side to side.

Again and again Miranda repeated the movement echoing the rhythm of the dildo, which Louisa was now energetically fucking. Within moments, Louisa cried out and clamped her thighs around Miranda's hand. Shuddering, she rode out her orgasm, finally sighing and letting her muscles relax.

She looked at Miranda and smiled. "Thank you, my dear friend. That was marvelous!"

Miranda smiled back.

That day had marked the beginning of a new phase of their sexual odyssey.

Now neither woman was hesitant about experimenting. Not just with the assorted sex toys either, but with each other and their bodies. Miranda learned what an orgasm should be, both with Louisa's fingers, her dildo, and finally, daringly, with Louisa's tongue.

They'd shared a bath before the fire in Miranda's room and had sneaked down to the secret passage late at night when the house had fallen quiet. A happy hour was spent laughing over the obscenely funny cartoons they'd found in a book by Rowlandson, but when they reached the one entitled "The Curious Parson", Miranda paused.

"He looks like he wants to eat her up, doesn't he?"

Louisa laughed. "He may well do so, my dear. Loving each other with tongues and mouths is a very pleasurable thing."

Miranda looked unconvinced, although she felt her arousal growing at the thought.

"Come, let me show you something," said Louisa, leading Miranda over to the chaise. "Settle yourself here, lean back and close your eyes. Keep them closed for me, promise?"

"I promise," giggled Miranda.

"Now think of the most handsome man you've ever seen…"

A vision of deep blue eyes and a sensual mouth flew into Miranda's mind. He'd been on horseback, passing her as she walked in the Park. His hair had flown free of its tie and it billowed around his shoulders like a black cloud of silk. His legs had been very muscular, flexing as they controlled his mount, and his eyes had met hers for less than a second, but she'd never forgotten him.

"All right, I'm imagining him," she breathed huskily.

"He is here, tonight, Miranda. He has come to worship at your body's altar." Delicate fingers opened Miranda's night robe and spread it wide, allowing the cool night air to caress her flesh.

Little kisses fell on each nipple and were followed by a progression of light bites down past her navel.

"That tickles, Louisa…"

"Shush! I am not Louisa tonight, I am he for whom you yearn," she scolded.

Hands stroked inner thighs and Miranda couldn't help but spread them wider. She felt a little tug and found herself being eased down slightly into a reclining position.

She jumped at the first touch of warmth against her pussy. "Oh God!"

"Hush now, he will be loving your sweet cunny, Miranda. Just relax and feel what his lips and tongue are doing."

Miranda lapsed back into her fantasy. His head was between her thighs now, she could feel his hair brushing her over-sensitive skin, his breath feathering her tissues.

She felt the moisture gather as her body became incredibly aroused from the vision in her mind.

Then—a quick stroke of a tongue.

She gasped aloud.

It came again and she felt her pelvis thrust towards the source. She rammed her spine against the cushions.

"Relax," came Louisa's soothing voice. "Let your body do as it will…"

Another stroke, this time lingering around her swollen clit. Then back away and down to capture her juices, which were starting to run freely.

She moaned.

The tongue was back, this time with serious intent. Swirling and lapping and teasing and flicking, it was sending Miranda into a tormented and frenzied arousal. She felt hands gripping her nipples and twisting them, the almost-pain adding to the fireworks that were sending her body into ecstasy and her mind into oblivion.

Suddenly the tongue plunged deep into her cunt, at the same moment as a hand pushed down on her clit.

The sensations overwhelmed her and she cried out, her cunt contracting violently and her muscles locked.

Louisa soothed her and brought her down from the peak, gentling her with words and strokes until the trembling ceased.

"He did a good job, didn't he?"

Miranda sighed and opened her eyes. "He did indeed, Louisa. He did indeed."

She never mentioned the name of her fantasy lover to Louisa, but the fates had conspired in their wondrous way, and now she was on her way to his home. Whether she could get Nick Barbour to suck her clit like that would be a matter of conjecture, but the fact remained—she was on her way to try and seduce the one man who had touched her soul.

* * * * *

Lord Nicholas Barbour loved his library. It was his office, his reading room and his sanctuary on nights like this when his partying friends were probably going to remain in their inebriated and naked state of lust until the early morning hours. At which point servants would shovel them (and their clothing if it could be found) into the nearest guest room. Sometime tomorrow several really bad headaches would stagger out of several guest rooms and painfully make their way to the breakfast parlor, trying not to vomit up the enormous amounts of alcohol they'd imbibed the night before.

There was no doubt in Nick's mind how special this room was. It was off-limits to his guests and his servants, only his long-time friend and valet, Jibber Potts, was allowed the privilege of entering. Jibber was fully aware of the cachet this distinction brought to him, and he jealously guarded the room from all who would try and get a prohibited peek.

Tonight there were flames leaping in the fireplace, his favorite wine in a decanter by his chair, and some soft blankets on the sofa. More often than not this was where Nick ended up sleeping.

The French doors were uncurtained and allowed a little moonlight to dapple the intricate parquet floor and the soft carpet. It was a scene of quiet contentment, and Nick slid out of his shirt and into his dressing gown with a sigh of relief.

Tonight's festivities had been just another in a series of unrelentingly boring orgies. He must be getting old, or jaded, or just plain fed up with life. Nick poured a glass of wine and felt his shoulders sag. He was miserable, and he knew it.

"Would you care to make that two glasses?"

Nick froze as a voice like honey swam through the silence and tapped him on the shoulder.

He turned slowly—and nearly dropped his wineglass.

She stood in the open French door, silhouetted by the moonlight. From the top of her carelessly coiffed flaming red hair to the tips of her shoes, she was magnificent. Clad all in black, the white mounds of her breasts were close to overflowing the inadequate dress and begging for some man's hands to set them free. She was masked, but the firelight danced from emerald green depths, and her generous lips curved in a smile.

She was very tall—Nick was over six feet and she was practically eye-to-eye with him. He couldn't restrain the thought that she was made for him to fuck. They'd fit perfectly.

His cock did something unusual. It twitched.

Refusing to reveal any inner turmoil, Nick casually put his glass back on the sideboard.

"And you are?"

"Here to fuck you, of course."

His cock twitched again. Nick blinked.

"Of course." Nick breathed slowly, trying to marshal his thoughts that were now all over the place, although mostly trying to get up inside this woman's skirt. Time to take control of this conversation.

"I shall look forward to it, My Lady…" his lips curved as he stared at her standing in the windows. "My Lady Moonlight. Won't you come in?"

He held out his hand and she moved forward with a confident step to place hers in it. He could feel her jump as their skin met and produced a definite tingle.

"My name is Miranda."

"*O brave new world, that has such creatures in it…*" quoted Nick softly.

Miranda's eyebrows rose. "Actually, I believe Miranda herself said that," she tilted her head slightly.

"Perhaps I should have said '…*if a virgin, and your affection not gone forth, I'll make you the queen of Naples…*'"

Miranda chuckled. "No crown, thank you, Lord Nicholas. I am here of practical necessity."

Nick sighed. "The money, is it?"

"Of course."

"You need the money badly enough to come into a strange house, offer to fuck the owner and then quote Shakespeare to him?"

"I do," she answered.

Nick shrugged. "Well, then, let's have at it, shall we?" His hands went to the belt of his robe and he unfastened it, surprised to note that his cock was already erect and indicating its readiness for the fun to start.

Miranda's eyes fell to his enormous arousal and she bit her lip.

"Intimidated?" he inquired.

"Impressed," she answered.

"In a hurry?"

"In a minute…"

She closed the doors behind her and moved to the sideboard. Her body shone like dark ebony in the velvet gown and Nick wanted nothing so much as to strip it off her.

"Why are you here? I know you're going to fuck me and so on, but why here and why now?"

"I was invited," she answered simply, pouring a second glass of wine.

"By whom?"

"Honestly? I don't know. Someone who knew I needed money, obviously, and someone who signed themselves 'a friend'. Other than that, I can tell you nothing."

"Yet you knew about this room, that I'd be here alone…"

"Apparently this friend is a mutual one. All that information was contained in the letter. Would you care to read it for yourself?"

She touched the wine to her lips, sipped, and then put it back down.

Nick shook his head. "No. I'd rather hold on to the illusion that you are here because you were summoned by my imagination…and my desires."

He reached out to her and stroked a hand over her cheek and down to her cleavage. Her skin was as soft as it appeared, yet there was a vibrant warmth beneath the surface. The green eyes widened and her pupils grew large at his touch.

Unable to wait, Nick dropped his robe to the floor, letting the heat from the fire warm his body.

Miranda licked her lips slowly. "*I might call him a thing divine, for nothing natural I ever saw so noble,*" she quoted softly as her eyes flickered over him.

Nick grinned.

"*Oh most dear mistress, the sun will set before I shall discharge what I must strive to do,*" he quoted back suggestively.

She drew even nearer, and Nick was convinced that the heat from his body must have been scorching her more than the warmth from the fireplace.

"*Admir'd Miranda,*" he breathed as she closed the space between them, stopping with her breasts just touching the hardness of his chest. "*So perfect and so peerless…*"

His words trailed off into silence as Miranda leaned towards him and brought her lips to his.

Chapter 3

She tasted of wine and honey and something indefinable that caught at Nick's desire.

He wanted nothing more than to seize her up close to him and rip her dress off, his instincts shrieking at him that he had to get this woman closer and he had to take her *NOW!*

Surprisingly, something stayed his urgency. Her lips were soft on his, her mouth warm and willing, and her tongue sweetly dueling with him. However, there was an innocence mixed in with the kiss, a curiosity of sorts, which Nick found very arousing, and *very* interesting.

His cock strived to find itself a snug harbor in the body of the woman and moved urgently against the velvet of her gown.

Her muted gasp of surprise was accompanied by the distinct pebbling of her nipples, which were now digging into Nick's chest. It was the most erotic moment he could remember in a long time, knowing his desires were inflaming a woman who was simply enjoying kissing him.

A slight smile crossed his features, and he decided that perhaps on this occasion, he'd let the lady hold the reins. She seemed in no rush to move forward with this seduction, simply relishing the games their lips and tongues were playing. He firmed his tongue and darted it in and out of her mouth in a parody of the lovemaking he intended would follow.

She caught his tongue with hers and tried to hold it, curling around him and establishing an amazingly sweet suction.

Nick barely repressed a shudder of need.

He sensed her arousal growing. Her body's particular fragrance was starting to permeate the air and mix with the light touch of florals she'd brought into the room with her. Her hips were moving ever so slightly—she might not even have realized she was doing it, mused Nick.

The part of him that remained uninvolved when it came to fucking was still functioning, but struggling...he was astounded by the level of excitement he'd reached by means of a simple kiss. He wondered if this might be something special, if *this* might be the night—if Miranda might be the one!

* * * * *

Miranda's head was floating. Never had she realized that the touch of lips could be so incredibly arousing. Nick's mouth was loving hers and hers was loving him right back!

His lips were firm and demanding and his tongue was playing one minute and seducing the next. He tasted of wine and man and a sweetness that took her breath away and made her pussy ache for his cock.

She was oh-so-ready to rip off her dress and let her nipples graze his chest. Indeed they were begging for his hands and his mouth and finding their velvet constriction almost painful.

Dragging in a breath, she fought for control. This was not how she had imagined the seduction. She had to pull back a little before her instincts got in the way of her plan. She knew now that she could arouse Nick—it was time to move on to the next stage. She had to learn whether he'd respond to other kinds of stimuli.

She raised her arms around him and put her hands low on his back, just above his buttocks. They felt warm and solid, and it was no hardship to slide her palm over one muscular globe. She dug her fingernails in slightly.

His cock jumped.

She smiled.

With her other hand she smacked his beautifully rounded bottom. Hard.

Nick jerked, and so did his cock.

"What do you think you're doing?" he asked, voice rough with need.

"Experimenting," she answered.

"On my backside?"

"I can't imagine anywhere better just at this moment," she murmured.

A cautious look of interest in Nick's midnight blue eyes encouraged Miranda, and she pulled away from him, noting the glistening drop of moisture that beaded the top of his huge cock. She brushed it away with fingers that trembled a little as she raised them provocatively to her lips. She sucked them with pleasure.

"Don't move, My Lord," she said, walking around him slowly.

"I have no intention of moving, My Lady."

Miranda raised her skirts behind Nick and pressed her mound against his naked buttocks.

He drew in a breath of surprise and reached out to hold the surface of the sideboard as she rubbed herself over his cheeks.

"That feels splendid," he encouraged. "Please continue this experiment of yours...anywhere else you'd like to rub your pussy?"

Unseen by Nick, Miranda blushed.

"Not quite yet, My Lord..."

"I think you probably should call me Nick, don't you? After all, that is my arse you're getting friendly with..."

"Very well, *Nick*..." a sharp slap punctuated Miranda's comment.

Nick groaned but stayed exactly where he was.

"And you..." *slap,* "may call me..." *slap,* "Miranda!" The final slap left a pink handprint across Nick's firm and tanned buttock, and brought a moan to his lips.

"God, how did you...why are you doing this..."

"'Tis whispered that a man often likes to be reminded that he too can feel. Sometimes pain is the answer..."

She knelt behind him and carefully shrugged her dress down off her shoulders, freeing her arms from the soft velvet.

"Sometimes 'tis pleasure..."

She rubbed her breasts back and forth across Nick's flushed and tingling buttocks, caressing him with her nipples and teasing him with the softness of her flesh.

Another moan told her that her actions were succeeding.

She wrenched herself away from the tempting mounds, leaned forward, sank her teeth into one luscious cheek and sucked, marking him with a faint bruise.

Nick writhed beneath her mouth, as she alternately sucked, nipped and licked his buttocks.

Then she pulled back and slapped him hard once more.

His head jerked back and he groaned, fingers turning white against the mahogany of the sideboard. His grip must have been ferocious because every muscle in his arms was quivering.

"You'll lose your ten thousand pounds any second now, My Lady," he hissed between clenched teeth.

"I don't think so, Nick," she breathed, letting him feel the velvet of her gown as it crumpled between them and fell to her feet.

He grunted as she again thrust her mound against him, letting him know that this time, she was standing nude behind him.

"I want to see you."

"I know."

"I'm going to turn around..."

"Not yet, My Lord. There are treats to come if you obey me," she ran her hand softly and caressingly across his buttocks, sliding lower and lower until he couldn't stop himself from spreading his legs and giving her access to his balls. They were hanging full and tight and he flinched when she lightly ran her fingertips across them.

She stood up tall behind him and pressed herself against his warmth, sliding one hand around to find and fondle his flat nipple.

"Oh God, Miranda," he sighed.

* * * * *

He wanted her—badly. He wanted her now. This very minute. Actually two minutes ago would be even better. If he didn't get her, he was going to come all over the Hepplewhite sideboard, and Jibber would never forgive him.

She was moving behind him, wriggling, fidgeting. He knew her gown had dropped to the floor because his sensitized body had marked the soft caress of its passage. Her mound was thickly covered with curls—were they as red as her hair? He couldn't wait to find out, especially since she'd brushed them over his buttocks, probably not realizing she'd left a trace of her juices there as well.

Oh yes, he wasn't the only one heating up with desire!

Now what was she doing?

He drew in a breath as he felt something cool and firm pass around his body. It was a drawstring, a belt, a lace perhaps? He looked down to see a pair of elegant white hands holding a black cord taut and nearing his cock.

Under his astounded gaze, the hands looped the cord around the thickness of his distended cock and slid it tight against his groin.

Then pulled on either end.

Nick clenched his teeth, but there was little pain, just an amazing feeling of sensual restraint and an overwhelming need to come.

"Turn around, Nick."

The whispered command caught him by surprise, and for a moment or two he had trouble releasing his death grip on the furniture.

Then his errant muscles began to function again, and he turned to face his sensual tormenter.

She stood proud in front of him in all her naked glory. Her breasts thrust out at him, as if defying him to use them as he wished. Nipples bunched tight, areoles darkened, her body whispered of its arousal to his waiting senses.

His gaze dropped to her crotch and he couldn't stop the grin from escaping as he saw the fiery mass of red curls that were hiding her secrets. And not doing a very good job of it, either, to judge by the little drops that sparkled amidst the rumpled pelt.

He noticed her stockings, still on her legs, and somehow the black silk and the little garters added an erotically striking note to this incredible woman. Her attentions were reducing him and all his preconceived notions about himself to a pile of whimpering need.

"Miranda...let me take you..." His cock strained against her as she swayed across his chest, rubbing herself over him like a cat in heat.

Her eyes were closed and she had obviously abandoned herself to the pleasure of feeling his touch all across her most sensitive places.

She retained her grip on the cord, however, and Nick hoped she wouldn't pull too much tighter – he was almost ready to burst as it was.

"Come, My Lord," she said, tugging gently on the cord.

"I'd like to," hissed Nick, following her towards the couch with teeth clenched and thighs knotted. "Let the damn cord go, and I'll come wherever and whenever you want. Soon. Probably very soon. In fact within seconds…"

Miranda giggled, a girlish sound that seemed surprising, given that it was coming from a naked red-haired goddess who'd gotten his cock tangled up in a black silk cord.

"Patience, Nick, patience," she murmured, running her hands over his iron-hard arousal. "How lovely you are…I think such magnificence deserves a kiss…"

Nick groaned, knowing he was finished if she put her lips anywhere near his throbbing length.

She did.

He was finished.

Or so he thought.

At the very last moment, Miranda tightened the cord to the point of pain. Nick climaxed, shuddering and thrusting, but nothing happened. No come spurted from his cock, which remained pretty much erect, happy, and ready to go again!

"Wha…" stuttered Nick.

"A simple technique, My Lord. It delays the emission of your semen, yet allows you to experience the pleasures of a climax."

Nick's lips curled in distaste.

"A whore's trick? Just who the hell are you, lady?"

"No whore, My Lord. That I can attest. I am merely well read, and of a curious mind. Perhaps my choice of literature might offend some, but I have learned much from my researches about how our bodies work, especially when a man and a woman are about to fuck each other."

Nick found himself believing her. Looking down into her green eyes, sparkling at him from beneath her mask, he could sense the honesty in her speech.

"Am I not to have the pleasure of fucking your cunt, then, Miranda?" he inquired. "You know that that is the basis for the release of funds *to* you…my release of come *within* you…"

His blunt words obviously embarrassed her and she blushed, surprising Nick yet again.

"We shall indeed fuck, Nick," she whispered, untying the cord from around his cock and running her tongue over the slight indentation it had made in his skin.

He moaned.

"Perhaps we are almost there..." she added.

Nick heartily agreed.

Chapter 4

Miranda was having a very big problem. She wanted nothing more than to knock Nick Barbour off his feet, stretch him out on the beautiful, soft Oriental carpet and fuck him 'til his eyes rolled back in his head.

She had never imagined that touching a man like this could be so enormously arousing, nor had she imagined that Nick's body would be so attractive to her.

She wanted about a week or so to examine every little nook and cranny, from his slightly crooked toes to the scar just above one knee, to the hair that curled in his armpits, to the tumble of black hair at the top of his head. And if she could use her tongue to cover that territory it would be even better.

But she knew that it was time for the most important part of her seduction. She had to get Nick inside her and she had to get him to come. And if possible, she'd like to come with him. Why not try for the improbable?

She had maneuvered them to the long couch and the look in Nick's eyes told her she had to move along with her program or relinquish control of the game to him.

That would be unwise.

It was time to put her weeks of training to good use. Time to make Louisa proud, and time to remember that she had practiced for many happy hours with a *diletto* as large as Nick. There would be no problem taking him inside her eager cunt— the problem would be making sure he stayed there long enough to come.

Focusing her concentration on the man breathing heavily in front of her, Miranda lowered herself to the couch.

"Will you do me the honor of entering my body, Nick?" she whispered. "It is ready and waiting for you…"

She leaned back against a pile of cushions and raised an arm over her head, thrusting her breasts at him in invitation. It was a wanton pose, but at this point Nick didn't seem to care much.

His eyes were brilliant blue, his face had colored slightly with the rise of his arousal, and his cock was about as hard as it could possibly get without exploding.

Miranda swallowed, trying to hide her nervousness.

"I have a feeling the honor will be all mine, My Lady," answered Nick gallantly.

His eyes swept her naked body, bringing the color flushing to her breasts. He knelt by the couch and indulged himself by sucking a nipple into his mouth.

Miranda groaned. This was too wonderful.

His hand slid to her pussy, fingers playing, seeking, searching out her most tender and responsive flesh and finally strumming her clit with enough skill to make her whimper and wriggle beneath his pressure.

"Ah, the passion of redheads," he mumbled, slipping his tongue around her nipple and biting it gently.

"Nick, please…"

"Please what, My Lady? Should I spank your beautiful bottom too? Would you like that?"

He punctuated his words with little flicks of his fingers between her legs, finally sliding his hand around to caress her buttocks and the dark cleft that separated them.

"Or perhaps you'd prefer something a little more…personal…" he ran his index finger through her juices and up to her cleft where he pressed, just hard enough to enter her tight little anus.

She gasped, unbelievably aroused.

"Oh God, Nick, that feels…"

"Yes, doesn't it?" he grinned.

"Please, My Lord, I want you now…" moaned Miranda.

"The Lady's wishes are my commands." Nick moved away from her a little, spread her legs apart and readied himself to enter her, gripping his cock and just teasing her shining labia with its head.

"Wait…let me get comfortable," she mumbled, remembering that she must take control of this, if she was to succeed.

"I don't think waiting is in the cards, Miranda," bit out Nick as he watched her juices shining on his straining length.

"A moment, just let me…"

Miranda raised one leg and allowed it to rest on the back of the couch. She was completely open to Nick, who licked his lips at the sight of her fiery pussy so close to his deep purple cock.

Then she slid her other leg between his and urged him into a kneeling position.

He tilted his head slightly as she sprawled before him.

"Now, Nick, come in me now…"

* * * * *

Nick moved in for the thrust, and her inner thigh brushed his side. It was a soft touch, but unbearably erotic, and Nick gasped.

He placed his cock in her entrance and thrust.

Deep, deep, deeper still.

"Give me all of you, Nick. Don't stop…"

"God, Miranda," breathed Nick as his cock slid further and further into the warmest, tightest, wettest, silkiest cunt he'd ever invaded.

Their pubic hair tangled, and Nick's body rested flush with hers.

He was all the way in.

Nick was shocked into immobility.

He had filled Miranda with his cock, and if the wild joy in her eyes was anything to go by, he'd filled her with pleasure, too.

The two intertwined bodies remained still for long seconds, meshed together in desire, and joined by something more.

Miranda raised one hand and slid it behind her head. She untied her mask, held it out over the side of the couch and dropped it on the floor.

This final act of revelation was enough to tip Nick over the edge.

Blue eyes met and held green ones as Nick began to move. Slowly at first, hesitant lest he hurt her, Nick slid and rocked gently within Miranda. His body brushed her clit and her juices drowned his cock. She was hot, so hot and tight around him that he felt ready to burst.

Miranda, for her part, was in heaven. Nick's cock was everything Louisa had ever promised a man's cock should be— and more. She felt filled with him, yet wanted more. He was deep inside her yet she knew she could have taken him further had she needed to.

Her hands slid to her nipples and she moaned at their sensitivity.

Nick slipped a hand between them and brushed her clit, watching her body as it began to writhe in concert with his movements.

The tension between them was building rapidly, as Nick's thrusts were met by enthusiastic and welcoming parries.

It was a sensual duel, move and counter-move, feint, withdraw and thrust again.

Sweat built on Nick's body, and Miranda's breath was coming in little gasping pants as the scent of their arousal blended and merged into the firelight glow of the room.

The slap of Nick's balls against Miranda's flesh punctuated their lovemaking, as did the little moans that Nick's cock forced from Miranda's soul.

She was oblivious to everything but his body bringing her incredible pleasures—he knew nothing but the warm slickness that was squeezing his cock and taking him into new worlds of sensation.

Their pace increased and Nick knew he was near, yet every fiber in his body was urging him to prolong this amazing sensation.

Miranda sobbed aloud as she felt the first stirrings of her orgasm. She too wanted to keep this experience going for as long as possible.

But nature would win out over both their desires.

Nick's buttocks tightened and his lips grimaced tightly over his teeth as the first tingling ripples started low on his spine.

Miranda's breath left her lungs in a gasp as she too felt the beginnings of a mighty orgasm building low in her cunt and spreading to her clit, her stomach, every nerve in her body.

"Now, Nick…" she yelled.

"Yes…Miranda…*YES!*"

Lord Nicholas Barbour ended six years of sexual control by enjoying a ferocious orgasm and blasting his come in fountains from his body!

Inside Lady Miranda.

* * * * *

The room was full of daylight, the fire was out and the candles had long since gutted in their holders when Jibber Potts and Sir Harry Boyd grinned at each other then looked back at the tangle of naked limbs that sprawled across the couch in Nick Barbour's library.

The scent of sex was strong, and Lady Miranda Montvale's breasts bore signs of beard burn, as did her neck, her cheeks and the inside of her thighs. Jibber and Harry appreciated the tableau for a moment before covering Miranda modestly with a blanket.

Nick himself was snuffling quietly into Miranda's hair, his day-old growth snagging some red strands and pulling them across his lips. His mighty sword was now lying limp and at rest, and probably would have been snoring contentedly had it been given the opportunity to voice its sentiments.

"I think we can safely say that last night was a success, Jibber," grinned Harry.

"No arguments there, My Lord," nodded Jibber.

Nick opened one eye and gazed sourly at them.

"Go away!"

Miranda stirred and cuddled closer to Nick. His gaze softened and he tucked the blanket snugly around her shoulders.

She opened both eyes and gasped at the men standing beside the couch. She shrank back into Nick's warmth.

Nick sighed. "Miranda, may I present two intrusive scoundrels. Jibber Potts, who runs my life with an iron hand, and Sir Harry Boyd, who is a friend and will continue to remain one if he gets his arse out of here within the minute!"

Harry chuckled.

"Lady Montvale and I are acquainted..." he said.

"We are?" asked Miranda.

"You know me better by my title, I believe. Harold, Earl of Dunsmere, at your service, Madam." Harry swept his hand high and bowed elegantly.

Miranda sucked in a breath.

"You!" she spat, clutching the blanket and raising herself up on one arm. "You're the one who called in the vouchers on my house. You're the one who's been demanding money. If it wasn't for you I wouldn't have...I..." she paused, remembering where she was and whose arms were holding her tightly.

"Quite," said Harry succinctly.

Nick's eyes narrowed. "This was all a set up, wasn't it? To get Miranda into my bed?"

Harry and Jibber assumed expressions of innocence.

"Actually, my boy, it's been quite a while in the planning." Harry pulled a chair near to the couch and settled himself comfortably, quite unconcerned by the nakedness underneath the one blanket in front of him.

"I have a dear friend, Miss Louisa Cellini."

Harry ignored Miranda's start of surprise.

"Lousia told me a long time ago that she had met the right girl for you, Nick, and Louisa is an excellent judge of such things. It was rather annoying that you had gone and married old Montvale, Miranda, but as it happened, things worked out for the best. We just had to figure out a way to train you well enough to handle making love to Nick, and then put you in a position where you'd have to seduce him. Hence my financial wheelings and dealings. I don't, by the way, want Montvale. I just want Nick to be happy."

Miranda was dumbfounded. "Louisa knew?"

"Louisa knew you had a secret desire hidden in your heart, and she was pretty sure that Nick had something to do with it. You might have let his name slip, now and again?"

Looking back on the number of screaming climaxes she and Louisa had shared, Miranda had to admit it might well have been possible.

"So, I'm your secret desire?" murmured Nick, licking his way around her ear lobe.

"Hush, we'll talk in a minute," reprimanded Miranda.

"Nick too, was ripe for plucking," added Harry.

"No question about it," added Jibber. "Some years ago he come in from a ride all flushed and excited. Seems he'd a-passed some girl with red hair and the greenest of eyes. Went on about her for weeks, he did. Never could find her, though…"

It was Miranda's turn to raise an eyebrow at Nick, who surprised himself and everyone else by blushing.

"Would you two get the hell out of here? Miranda and I have some business to work out between us," snarled Nick, embarrassed now and wanting nothing more than Miranda. Alone, naked and ready for him.

Seeing as she was already two out of three, he knew that all he had to do was rid the room of the tenacious vermin that wouldn't go away!

"We're gone," laughed Harry, heading for the door.

"Welcome to the family, My Lady," smiled Jibber, following Harry.

Silence fell, while Nick looked at Miranda, and Miranda looked anywhere but at Nick.

"How did you do it, Miranda?"

She knew exactly what he was asking.

"It was Louisa. After Montvale died, I found a room where he had stored any number of…of sex toys." Her white skin flushed as she told her tale, and Nick gently ran his fingers up and down her arm, making her shiver.

"She showed me how to use them and how to enjoy myself and my body. That's what gave me the courage to come here with the knowledge that I could take you completely inside me."

She reached down and stroked him cautiously, grinning as she felt him waking to vibrant life beneath her fingers. "Did you know that a woman expands to take her man? That there's a small place next to my womb where only the biggest cock can touch?"

Nick was losing track of the conversation. The blanket was slipping and he wanted nothing more at that moment than to be where he'd been most of the night.

Inside Lady Miranda.

Epilogue

Sir Harry Boyd watched with pride as Lady Miranda Montvale exchanged vows with Lord Nicholas Barbour and ended the silly bet. White's had already removed the offending pages from their betting book and marked them "closed".

Montvale House had been deeded over to Louisa for her lifetime, and for that alone, Harry could have hugged Nick and Miranda. Louisa was a special friend and deserved her reward.

To judge by the look in Nick's eye, there'd be a parcel of little Barbs on the way soon, thus ensuring the continuation of the line and the end of "Barbour's Follies", as Harry had come to think of Nick's orgies.

Harry sighed.

He knew at some point he'd have to take the plunge, but not, by God, until he was ready. And not until he found the right woman.

If such a creature even existed.

In the meantime, Lady Mary Calthorpe was eyeing him with great interest, and she was reputed to have magnificent nipples that swelled to the size of grapes when she was being fucked. Perhaps it was time he researched that particular claim.

Nick Barbour looked deep into the eyes of the woman who was now his wife and cupped her cheek with his hand.

"With a heart as willing as bondage e'er of freedom: here's my hand," he said, knowing she would recognize Ferdinand's speech as he professed his love for his Miranda.

"And mine with my heart in't," she quoted back, her love glowing from every pore.

"You know where I'm going to spend the rest of my life, don't you?" he whispered.

She raised an eyebrow at him.

"Inside Lady Miranda!"

MISS BEATRICE'S BOTTOM

Chapter 1

The bruise on Beatrice Shelton's cheek ached as she dressed herself in the darkness of her tiny room. Other parts of her body were no better. The welts across her shoulders stung, although she knew she'd been lucky that no skin had been broken.

Her most private areas throbbed from the manhandling they'd received, but once again she thanked heaven that her father had interrupted the curate before he'd torn off all his vestments and raped her.

Of course her father was now convinced that she was a fallen woman, unfit for the company of other humans, and treated her as such. All because a weak man couldn't keep his hands to himself.

The numbing cold made tying laces almost impossible, and Beatrice barely managed to slip her feet into her old boots. The holes that had worn through the soles would make walking difficult, but walk she must!

Easing her way out of her room, she clutched her little bundle of belongings tightly inside her cloak and slipped down the back stairs. The third one squeaked—she stepped gingerly over it.

The back door would be the biggest obstacle. It was bolted with a mighty iron rod that Beatrice's small fingers would have a hard time unlatching, but she was determined to try. No longer would she stay in this cold and forbidding house, subject to her father's beatings and his total domination.

After agonizing minutes of fighting the bolt, cold fresh air flowed into the kitchen and Beatrice stepped outside with a sigh of relief.

Cautiously closing the door behind her, she set off into the darkness. It would be hours before sunrise, and she had a strong feeling that snow might well obscure the coming of day anyway.

But it didn't matter. She had escaped. Miss Beatrice Shelton, daughter of the Vicar of Lyndenham, was free.

* * * * *

Sir Harold Boyd, Earl of Dunsmere, was whistling happily to himself as he rode down the quiet country lane. It was early morning, and the snow had held off until he was but a few miles from his destination where he knew a warm welcome would be awaiting him.

Montvale House and Louisa Cellini were getting nearer with each hoof beat, and Harry grinned over his horse's ears at the thought. Although Nick and Miranda Barbour weren't visiting at the moment, Louisa would be there. She was always there—it was her house now. Several years older than Harry's thirty-seven summers, Louisa had absolutely no interest in him sexually. He still hadn't decided whether to be offended or not, even though he'd known Louisa for a long time.

But she was one hell of a companion, and her company was worth so much more than a quick fuck any day. God knew he'd had enough of those. Her conversation was intelligent, occasionally quite risqué, she was extraordinarily well read, and she could play the meanest hand of cribbage this side of anywhere on earth. He'd had enough of being pursued by marriage-minded women, and a surfeit of fucking non-marriage-minded women. This little holiday was just what he needed. The food at Montvale was excellent, the staff friendly and efficient, and right now Harry couldn't think of anyplace else he'd rather be.

Consequently, he wasn't in the least prepared for what looked like a snow-covered angel to appear in the lane before him, holding out one blue-white hand in mute appeal.

Harry's horse stopped dead, and Harry's tuneful whistle was strangled by a gasp of surprise.

"S...s...sir..."

The apparition tumbled into a heap on the ground.

Harry didn't move. Surely angels flew. They shouldn't flop into a pile of old clothing, or — he noticed — be wearing boots with holes in them.

Conclusion? This was not an angel, but someone in dire need of help.

Dismounting, he cautiously approached the lump on the path.

"Hello?" He nudged it with his toe. It had looked like a woman, but one could never be too sure these days. Harry spared a glance around, his mind already alert to the very real possibility that others might be lurking in the shadows, waiting to take advantage of an unwary Samaritan.

Under his prodding boot the body rolled, and Harry gasped.

Masses of straight blonde hair fell free from a rather disreputable hat and framed a face that could well have come to life from any stained glass window in any church in the land. That was, of course, an assumption, seeing as it was doubtful that Harry could remember what the inside of a church looked like, let alone a stained glass window.

Odd thoughts cascaded through his mind as he bent to examine his surprising find.

She was nearly dead with cold, that much was certain, and although he could feel a pulse fluttering in her neck, her flesh was much too clammy and white and her lips were colorless.

Harry dashed back to his horse and unstrapped his extra greatcoat, blessing his valet for insisting he take it.

Readying himself for the effort, Harry bent to the woman, only to find she weighed next to nothing. Her apparent bulk came from her shapeless cloak and a bundle she clasped tightly, even in her unconscious state. Within moments he'd wrapped her up, bundle and all, in his coat and had used a handy log to get them both back onto his mount.

"Well, Miss Angel, let's see if Louisa can warm you up a bit. Please just hold on—we'll get you out of this very soon."

His voice must have percolated through her daze, because for a moment her eyelids flickered and she stared at him.

Harry's breath stopped as he gazed into a pair of magnificent sea-blue eyes.

"I'm going to die, aren't I?" she muttered through frozen lips.

"Not if I have anything to say about it," answered Harry, holding her as close as he could and snuggling his cloak around both of them.

"I don't mind. It'll be better than before. And if everyone looks like you, I'll be happy in heaven. You're beautiful..."

Her voice trailed off and her eyes closed again.

Harry put the spurs to his horse and flew recklessly through the snowflakes that had begun to fall. There was a lump in his throat that threatened to choke him, and a frantic desire to save this woman's life.

The pounding of his horse's hooves was no louder than the pounding of his heart as he hugged his fragile burden. Thinking back over the women he'd taken to his bed, he couldn't recall a moment when he'd felt *this* particular way. He'd taken pride in the title "rake," and earned it between more thighs than he could remember. So why did a couple of simple words from this frozen angel tie his heart in knots when all the fucking he'd done with all those beautiful women had left him untouched?

It was absurd, it was wonderful, and it settled deep in his loins and burrowed into his soul.

She'd called him beautiful.

Chapter 2

Louisa Cellini shook her head at Harry's unvoiced question. They were both standing next to the bed in one of Montvale's guest rooms where a fire was roaring and the air was so warm it practically shimmered.

"I do not know, dear Harry. She was chilled quite to the bone. Her heartbeat is strong, but her body..." Louisa shook her head again.

"What's wrong with her body?" asked Harry, puzzled.

"Look and see," said Louisa, raising the blankets away from the woman lying unconscious on the bed.

She was face down, and it was easy to see why.

Harry's breath hissed through his teeth, and his gut clenched as he saw the welts that criss-crossed her white shoulders. There was some light bruising further down, and as Louisa continued to reveal her skin, Harry saw the distinct marks of fingers on the white of her bottom.

And what a bottom it was.

Twin creamy white mounds jutted away from her body, shaped to fit a man's hand. Firm, succulent flesh, separated by a sculptured cleft hinting at a woman's secrets and undiscovered sources of pleasure.

Harry couldn't help himself. He stretched out his hand and gently smoothed one of her buttocks. Her skin was softer than the finest velvet, and Harry found himself instantly hard. He fought against the urge to follow her crease down to the shadows between her legs. She was unconscious and injured, for heaven's sake! What manner of man was he to even think of such a thing? He was a man seduced by a beautiful bottom, that's what he was.

Irritated at himself, he turned to Louisa.

"So you don't know if she'll survive?"

"There is more, Harry. Look here." Once again, Louisa bent to her patient and rolled her gently onto her side.

The woman groaned slightly and settled herself more comfortably.

Harry wished he could do the same, but his cock was threatening to jump right through his breeches as his eyes devoured the naked body sprawled before him.

He dragged his attention away from her small but firm breasts, down the milky line of her body to where Louisa was pointing.

Her upper thighs were badly bruised, along with some smaller markings just inside her lower hip.

"She has been mauled, my friend. And very roughly."

"Was she raped, do you think?" asked Harry, rage flooding his veins.

"I do not know, but I think perhaps not..." Louisa bit her lip with a worried expression on her normally calm face.

"There was no evidence of such an attack, and these bruises are new, perhaps as recent as yesterday. I do not know her, nor does my staff. If...when she awakens we'll have more information. Until then, it will be in God's hands. I have done all I can..."

Louisa swayed slightly.

"Louisa?" Harry was instantly at her side.

"Forgive me, Harry, I believe I may have a touch of the ague. Perhaps you'd be so kind as to watch our patient for a while? I find I must rest, then I can stay with her tonight..."

* * * * *

The room was dark but for two small candles and the glowing fire.

Harry Boyd smiled as he imagined his friends' surprise could they see him at this moment, playing nurse to an unconscious woman.

Louisa had slept the day away and Harry had refused to let anyone wake her, insisting on staying with their unknown patient himself. He'd changed into his dressing gown, helped himself to a decanter of Louisa's very fine brandy and was now toasting himself and his toes simultaneously.

A groan from the bed snapped his attention back to the woman, and he stood quietly, listening.

"No, please…"

The mutter was soft but clear.

She was either dreaming or feverish, thought Harry. He moved to stand next to her bed.

"No, I don't want…"

Her head tossed back and forth on the pillows, making it hard for Harry to touch it and judge her body's temperature. Instead, he placed his hand on her neck in that delicate spot where her muscles joined and the skin was so soft. Her pulse pounded beneath his fingers, but she did not feel unduly heated.

"Don't do that, I don't like it…" she gasped.

Harry jumped, then realized she was speaking to someone else, not him.

"So cold…"

She began to shiver. Great shudders wracked her delicate frame, and Harry glanced around for more blankets, something, anything to warm her up.

The fire blazed in the hearth and the room was already heated through. This chill came from inside her, not from outside. That was very clear.

Harry obeyed the promptings of his inner demons and told himself that his actions were sensible under the circumstances.

Promising to engage in a stern inner dialogue very shortly, Harry dropped his robe and clambered under the covers next to her, pulling her into the warmth of his naked body.

Instinctively, she turned and wriggled close, seeking the heat of his skin next to hers.

Harry sucked in a breath.

This might not have been the best idea he'd ever had.

She fit into his arms like she'd been made for them. Her golden head rested on his shoulder and her small breasts pressed firmly into his chest. He gritted his teeth as her hand scrabbled around his sensitive nipple only to nuzzle its way into his armpit.

She lifted one leg and smoothed her thigh over his, just brushing his growing erection and bringing a groan to his throat.

He could feel her silky mound pushing against his hip, and his cock was now signaling a variety of needs, prime amongst which was to get inside this lovely little piece of womanhood he was cuddling.

She sighed as she rubbed her head against him.

Harry sighed as he refrained from rubbing his cock against her.

Long minutes passed, during which Harry sternly lectured himself and his baser urges.

Holding on to one of her beautiful breasts in order to prevent her from falling off the bed would not be a good idea. And there was no medical evidence to show that suckling on a sweet, budded nipple might help to check for a fever.

The memory of the bruises he'd seen on her body kept his touch delicate, but she was the damndest temptation he'd run across in a long time.

He tried to divert his thoughts from the soft whiteness of her skin.

Whiteness. Yes, soft and smooth, like his latest horse. That was it, think horses. The recent auction at Tattersall's had yielded the most delicate little filly for his stable, which would probably throw some fleet-footed racers after she was bred. With his stallion. His big stallion.

Who would have to mount her from behind.

Like he would like to do to his bedmate.

He'd like to raise her hips, tuck one or maybe two of those fluffy pillows underneath her and open her white thighs. Perhaps he'd tease her a little with his cock, running it up and down her cleft. Maybe a little love bite on that wonderful bottom of hers. Lots of licking.

He salivated.

What would her little tight ring of muscles do if he rubbed it gently with his cock while his fingers found her clit and urged it out to play?

His body ached, and he closed his eyes against the pain.

Horses, think of horses. No, that didn't work.

His holdings. He was an earl, dammit; he had responsibilities. Time to concentrate on some of them.

That property in Hampshire needed some attention.

Harry tried to recall his agent's letter suggesting they consider plowing up one of the meadows near the river for barley next year.

But then he remembered fishing in that particular spot, and how the wind rustled through the willows on the bank. How he'd love to take *her* there. Perhaps ease her out of her clothes and lay her on the shaded grass amidst the clover and the buttercups. One or two flowers in her shining woman's hair, to be removed by his willing mouth, drenched with her juices.

Oh, God. He was harder than iron.

She stirred, and when he looked down at her, he realized her eyes were open.

"You," she sighed.

"Yes, me."

"I'm dead, aren't I?"

"No, you're not dead. You're warm and safe and in my arms, and I'll never let anyone hurt you ever again." As soon as the words were out of his mouth he stopped, shocked. It was very unlike Harry Boyd to make such a blanket statement to a woman, let alone one he'd only met twelve hours before.

"You're still beautiful…" she whispered, pulling a hand free of the bedding and stroking his beard-roughened cheek.

There it was again. That wrenching lurch that caught him from his balls to his throat. He blinked, realizing that her touch was fanning his already primed desire for her.

Perhaps she would be shocked at these thoughts that he shouldn't be having. Perhaps her sea-blue eyes would turn stormy, and that delectable mouth might pout if she knew he wanted to bury his face in her clit and suck at it until she pounded her heels into his back with ecstasy.

How would she feel if he asked her to spread her legs and rest them on his shoulders while he thrust his tongue into paradise? Would she blush or smile at the notion that his taste buds were screaming for a taste of her nipples, which might well outrank the most delectable French cuisine?

Perhaps he should get out of this bed before she realized that there were three of them sharing the blankets. Him, her and his cock.

He drew a breath and attempted to calm his lust.

"What's your name?"

"Beatrice." Her hand followed his jaw down to his neck. Harry found it amazing that the touch of her hand on his face could cause a reaction somewhere quite different.

"*My dear Lady Disdain…*" The quote slipped from Harry's mouth before he'd thought about it.

The smile that crossed her face stopped his heart.

"*Courtesy itself must convert to Disdain if you come in her presence.*"

The answering quote threw Harry for a loop.

Her hand continued its journey across his chest, idly playing amidst the dark hairs that whorled around his nipples, then continuing on to the intriguing dip of his navel.

She was heading lower when he gently grasped her wrist.

"You are heading for dangerous territory, Beatrice," he breathed, as her blue eyes pinned him with a look of wonder.

"I am dead, sir. Thus I can be as dangerous as I desire. No harm can come to me now. "

Releasing her wrist, Harry let her have her way, and coincidentally began silently praying for control. Coming all over her hand would not add to her illusion of heaven.

Her arm stretched across him as she slipped her palm down over his abdomen and found the treasure she sought.

The combination of innocence and curiosity was almost too much for Harry, who nearly cracked a molar holding on to his control.

She grasped his cock gently and leaned her head on his chest as she considered the amazing organ within her hand.

"How smooth it is, yet how firm," she murmured.

"Um, yes," gasped Harry, frantically working his way through the multiplication tables.

Her fingers slid around the ridge and up to the small opening where a drop of moisture had gathered.

Harry's mind moved on to some particularly challenging Latin declensions.

She gently smeared the droplet of his come over the head with gentle swipes, concluding her creation with a flourish.

Greek verbs marched in formation through Harry's fragmented consciousness until her next words brought him back to reality with a thud.

Chapter 3

"He wanted to put this in me, you know," she said, tapping Harry's cock.

Harry turned to prayer.

"Who did, sweetheart?" he asked, stroking her hair off her forehead in a last-ditch effort to distract himself from the gentle torture her nimble fingers were inflicting.

"Papa's curate."

"Papa's...oh my God. You're a *Vicar's* daughter?" *That* pronouncement worked. Harry distinctly felt his cock shrink.

"I was—until I died. Now I am going to heaven, but I'm allowed to find out what I missed before I get there. You see, there's no—um—lovemaking in heaven," she said seriously, twirling some of Harry's pubic hairs playfully around her finger. "I always knew that I'd find out before I went to heaven. It seems as though so much time is spent on the subject that it would be silly to die and not experience it, don't you think?"

Her sea-blue eyes turned to Harry's, and he took a deep breath as her gaze restored all his vitality. His cock was raring to go again, but he knew he had to be patient. For once he was glad of his age and experience. Ten years ago he knew he'd have come twice already, just from being this close to a naked woman like Beatrice, let alone considering what she was doing to him.

She'd discovered his balls and was now eagerly exploring this new territory.

Harry suppressed a moan.

"Beatrice, can you tell me what happened?" he whispered, hoping perhaps to divert her away from that most sensitive portion of his anatomy.

"Mr. Phillipston said Papa told him I would wed him. So he saw no reason not to anticipate our wedding vows. He pulled up my skirt and poked at me with his hands and then he unlaced his britches, and…" She paused, hand stilled over his scrotum.

Harry scarcely breathed, waiting for her next words.

"And he took this part of himself from his breeches. It wasn't lovely, like yours, though…" She returned to her stroking and petting. "He had to pull at it to make it stand out. It was rather ugly. Yours is beautiful. But I suppose that's to be expected because angels are always beautiful. What saint sent you?"

Her gentle question caught Harry completely by surprise.

"I'm not…not what you think, Beatrice…" he stuttered, barely able to get the words out because she'd found that extra-sensitive spot beneath the end of his cock. She was delicately flicking it and sending his eyes rolling back into his head with pleasure.

"I know. *Saint Desiderare*. You are an emissary from the patron saint of Desire, are you not?"

Harry was reaching the end of his tether. He was trying to come clean with her, and all she was doing was making him want to come.

He took her hand and eased it away from his aching balls.

She swiftly looked up at him and tears filled her eyes. "Am I not worthy of experiencing pleasure, my Emissary?" she asked sadly.

Harry could no more have refused her than cut off his own cock with a butter knife.

"You are more than worthy, Beatrice. But I must be gentle with you—and remember you have suffered gravely at the hands of other men."

Harry continued to pray for patience. He wondered if it was because he was in bed with a vicar's daughter that he was suddenly experiencing this overwhelming need to seek guidance from a Higher Authority. He'd never needed to before.

A frown crossed Beatrice's face at his words. "Their hands, yes. Cruel hands. You know, my father beat me when he caught Mr. Phillipston under my skirt. He said I was a whore of the devil for tempting him."

Harry ground his teeth. "You are no whore, my lovely. Your father was wrong. So wrong. And so was Mr. Phillipston."

Another prayer—this time for the opportunity to meet both these men sometime soon. With a butter knife in hand and no one else in the vicinity. And the prayer wasn't to any patron saint, either. It went directly to whichever divine office handled painful retribution.

"Can I not know a woman's pleasure then, Sir Emissary?"

"Of course you can," chuckled Harry. It was a rather rusty sound, given that Beatrice had gone back to her previous occupation and was now swirling her little finger through another bead of moisture she'd found at the tip of his cock.

"But I shall not enter you, Beatrice. It would be...it is forbidden to me," said Harry, thinking that if sainthood was possible, he might just qualify right this minute.

"I understand, sir," replied Beatrice, lying back on the pillows expectantly.

The room was darkening as the fire died down, and Harry lost his breath for a moment at the sight of Beatrice's beautifully slender white body illuminated by the single candle that still burned.

"Should I do something? Am I not in the right place?" She fidgeted slightly under his intense gaze.

"You are perfect. Just perfect. Do not move a muscle." An idea popped into Harry's mind. "I must do penance for the injustice that you have received at the hands of those you should have been able to trust, Beatrice. I will show you a woman's pleasure, but in the way it should be between a man and a woman. I will make you forget that a man's hands can be used for anything other than caresses."

Beatrice thought about that for a moment. "That makes perfect sense. The saints are wise, are they not?" She smiled happily at him and wiggled her bottom a little, obviously ready for his attentions.

Harry wouldn't have been surprised to find his entire lower body engulfed in flames. He was hotter than hot, and wanted desperately to sink deep into Beatrice and never come out. He closed his eyes, offering one last prayer to Saint Gritted Teeth of the Delayed Come, asking for a blessing that would keep him from spurting his seed all over the white and gold body of this lovely woman. At least not yet!

"Let us try this," he murmured.

* * * * *

Beatrice struggled with two emotions.

The first was fear.

She was not unfamiliar with this feeling, but knowing she was on her way to heaven inspired a different kind of fear than she'd experienced while waiting for her father's blows. This was a tremulous kind of expectant fear. The kind of fear that was three parts anticipation and only one part terror.

The other emotion was purely sensual. For the second time this lovely angel with the meltingly dark eyes had looked at her and turned her heart upside down. She was so glad that he had been picked to initiate her into the mysteries of lovemaking.

She'd always known that there had to be somewhere between heaven and earth. As a child growing up listening to her father's sermons on sin and piety, Beatrice had become convinced that there had to be a place that was the opposite of purgatory. She'd begun to imagine it as sort of a coaching inn where souls on their way to the afterlife would stop and take care of their unfinished business. Although as an adult she'd not thought much about it, facing death by freezing had brought it back to her mind, and now here she was.

The touch of his tongue on her flesh drove out all other emotions as every inch of her skin reacted.

"Oh, my," she breathed, watching in fascination as his tongue traced her nipple and made it stand erect.

"Do you like that?" His voice was deep and husky, and she felt an ache begin way down deep inside her body.

"Oh yesssss…" she answered as tendrils of sensation ran from her nipples to her loins, and other places began thrumming with tension.

"Good," he muttered, turning his attention to her other breast with the same results.

She writhed as he continued to work slow magic with his tongue on various portions of her body. She'd never have guessed that her belly button was a screaming center of sensation, or that a quick lick with a wet tongue to the inside of the elbow could make her want to sigh and gasp out her surprise. She wriggled again, obeying an inexplicable urge to thrust her hips forward, searching, seeking for something. She had no idea what it was, just that the man touching her could give it to her.

She widened her eyes as he reached for the sheepskin blanket that was folded at the bottom of the bed.

"Turn over, Beatrice," he urged, helping her roll onto her stomach.

She rested her face on her crossed arms and waited, jittery and aware of his warmth. Her breasts felt swollen and tender as they pressed into the bedding, and her whole body trembled with expectancy.

Then something soft passed across her buttocks.

She jumped.

"Shhh…" came his voice soothingly. "Just close your eyes and feel…"

Doing as she was told, she jumped again as the softness of the sheepskin caressed her flesh. It was the most amazingly sensual feeling she'd ever experienced. Like letting the sunshine touch her bare skin, only better. Like a cool breeze blowing across her nakedness on a hot day, only better. Her thighs spread themselves without any conscious thought on her part, and again she felt the urge to thrust. But this time, she wanted more of that feather-light softness against her buttocks. She raised her hips slightly, encouraging his touch.

"Such a beautiful bottom," he said, following the skin with his tongue.

Oh, Lord. He was *licking* her. And it felt incredible. She wanted to shout the glory of it to the four corners of the world and coincidentally, she wanted to move to some rhythm that her body was starting to understand. She clutched at the sheets as she felt Harry's fingers gently ease her cheeks apart and stroke her tightly puckered anus. Her eyes opened wide and she gasped.

"Sir...should you...I mean..." she stuttered.

"Beatrice. Am I not your Emissary? Can you not trust me?"

"Oh yes. I'm sorry. Please—continue..." Beatrice lay back down, wondering if this incredible surge of feeling inside her body was normal. Her nipples were tight buds now, each movement rubbing them almost painfully. Her woman's mound was throbbing and she was one huge mass of yearning, scared of what might come next, but more scared that he'd stop before she found out.

His lips again caressed her, moving from her buttocks down her thighs and back up again. He punctuated his movements with little nips from his teeth, which set her skin on fire. The bedding beneath her mound became damp.

"Sir, I must mention. I grow wet in an unusual place. Is this customary?" Her voice was so quiet she wondered at first if he'd heard her embarrassed question.

"'Tis part of desire, my Beatrice, and I welcome it, as should you. Your body is telling me of its arousal and response to my deeds. I thank you for it," he answered formally, setting her mind to rest.

"Oh, well that's all right then," she said, and lay back once again on her hands.

He continued to lavish his attentions on her bottom, sometimes with his tongue, sometimes with the sheepskin, and sometimes with something else. Something that was warm yet velvety, hard and strong but surprisingly smooth. She bit her lip when she realized that he was rubbing '*that*' part of himself against her, and she was loving it. She reached back without a thought and eased her buttocks apart so that he could rub her more effectively.

She heard him moan softly and she shivered as he dipped himself into her juices and then ran his cock back up between her buttocks.

"Are you well, sir?"

"Are you mad, woman?"

Beatrice sucked in a breath, but he interrupted her before she could respond. "I am very well. Almost too well, Beatrice. Your bottom is a marvel of art, a magnificent example of nature's bounty."

Beatrice giggled and then a moan escaped her as he pressed himself tight against her sensitive muscles and clasped her thighs with his. The feel of his firm, hairy flesh pressing against her made her want to thrash and scream and cry out. Instead, she pressed her buttocks back into his groin.

"Sir," she panted, "I must tell you that what you are doing…"

"Yes, Beatrice?"

"What you are doing to me is most pleasurable…" She gasped and nearly choked as Harry reached beneath her to fondle her breasts.

"Please do not stop."

"Let me assure you," groaned Harry with feeling. "I have absolutely no intention of stopping. I couldn't stop if my life depended on it. In fact, I may never stop. You will be forced to remain beneath me for eternity."

This time, Beatrice's giggle was husky and sensual, and she was astounded that such a sound had come from her own throat.

"Then eternity it shall be," she sighed, easing her legs even wider apart. She wanted this, all of it, to take her wherever it would, to teach her what passion was. To take her to heaven at last.

Chapter 4

"Turn over once more, Beatrice-sweet," said Harry, knowing he could not go any further without embarrassing himself, and possibly destroying her illusion. The sound of her giggle had sent a bolt of lust through his body, but instead of rousing his cock to unheard of proportions, it had settled in the vicinity of his heart. It was a little disturbing, and Harry needed to get back to a place where he felt in control.

Bringing her to climax would be just the thing.

Probably.

Because if he didn't, he'd never forgive himself. After all, she thought he was a saintly emissary — he did have a reputation to maintain.

He eased the sheepskin underneath her as she turned so that the softness would cradle her body and add to the sensations she was already experiencing.

The scent of her arousal swirled around his head like fumes from an opium pipe, with equally addictive results. Harry knew he'd never be able to rid himself of this particular fragrance. For a fleeting moment, he wasn't sure if he wanted to.

"I am going to make you fly, Beatrice," he whispered, letting the warmth of his breath dust her sweet pussy.

She sucked in her breath and grasped the bed linen with her hands.

"Very well, sir. I am ready." She closed her eyes and braced herself against what was to come.

Harry grinned to himself, then bent his head to her soaking flesh.

One taste of her juices and Harry was lost. He licked and slurped and teased and flickered, running from her streaming cunt to her swollen clit and back, listening with glee to her moans and gasps as he worked her tissues into a frenzy.

Staying true to his word, he used his hands ever so gently, even when the urge to grip her beautiful buttocks hard and raise her to his mouth was pressing indeed!

He did allow himself the luxury of gently resting his forearms over her thighs, which helped to hold her in place and open her even more to his attentions. He made sure to avoid the bruises on her soft flesh, but just seeing them from the corner of his eyes made him redouble his efforts to bring her pleasure.

Her soft golden mound glittered with a blend of her own juices and his saliva — he couldn't believe the effect this one little woman was having on him.

He'd done this many times to many women, but never had he enjoyed it more, nor had he ever seemed unable to get enough of the taste he craved.

Beatrice's groans of delight added to Harry's pleasure, and when he heard her breath start coming in shorter and shorter gasps he knew she was close. He gently continued his endeavors, adding a quick lick down to her cleft for good measure.

But always her scent and her little bud of desire drew him back. Her flesh was swollen and hot and her clit had thrust out from under its protective hood. Harry knew it would be too sensitive for him to suckle, much as he wanted to.

He contented himself with firm strokes all around, and judging from her sounds, that was just fine with Beatrice.

Her hands tightened on the bed sheets, and Harry felt the muscles of her thighs harden under his arms.

"Ohgodohgodohgod..." she breathed.

"Yes, Beatrice, yes..." urged Harry, burying his face in her cunt and shoving his tongue as far into her as he could go.

He moved his face slightly and felt her break.

Her soft scream of pleasure coincided with the most violent contractions he'd ever felt, and he could not resist raising his head and quickly shoving two fingers as far inside her as he could.

Watching Beatrice as she writhed in the paroxysms of pleasure around his hand was an amazing experience that knocked Harry's world off its foundations.

Her body flushed; her nipples stood firm and sharp at the tips of her swollen breasts. Her slender stomach moved in time with her muscle spasms and even her toes were curling. She was so totally involved with her orgasm that Harry just sat and watched, spellbound by what he was seeing.

He gently pulled his hand away from her as she began to unwind from her sexual frenzy.

Beads of her moisture fell from his fingers onto his arousal, and he was lost.

With fingers still covered with Beatrice's juices and Beatrice's scent surrounding him, he grabbed his cock and in no more than three or four firm strokes, brought himself to climax.

For the first time in more years than he could remember, thirty-seven year old Harry Boyd, Earl of Dunsmere, spent himself all over his hand.

Chapter 5

Three months later

"She wants to *what*?" Sir Harry Boyd's voice was only a few degrees shy of a shriek.

"Quiet, my friend. I do not wish her to know you are here," chided Louisa.

The two stood near a window, watching a slight blonde figure walk sedately over the well-tended paths to a gate at the end. Her golden curls peeped out from under her bonnet and were stirred by the light breeze. She was a picture of rural innocence and even from this distance, Harry's mouth watered and his cock stirred restlessly.

Louisa quietly noted his reactions but held her tongue, merely answering his question. "She wishes to enter a convent."

"That's what I thought you said." Harry shook his head in disbelief. "Why?"

Louisa sighed. "Come, sit down, Harry. Let me tell you about Beatrice, and perhaps together we can decide how to handle this situation."

Harry willingly sat, his attention riveted on the woman opposite him.

"She recovered well from her ordeal in the cold, although she seemed convinced she had died for a period of time. She kept mentioning an Angel of Desire, or some such fancy..."

Harry coughed, politely turning his head away from Louisa for a moment.

He missed the little grin that passed over her elegant features.

"Anyway, she soon realized she was not dead, but still alive. It took but a little time for her to unburden herself, and it was as I told you in my letters. She'd been kept in dire straits by that insane father of hers; whether for religious or simply mad reasons I have no idea. But her attack by that curate fellow was the last straw and drove her out of Lyndenham into the storm. And, coincidentally, into your arms."

Harry fought a surprising blush.

"Since then, we have worked on healing her body and her mind. The scars have disappeared from her flesh, but I believe there is still a mark on her spirit. She believes herself unworthy of a man's love and yet is angry enough to declare she will never give herself to any man. It is a conflict within her, I think."

Louisa paused, collecting her thoughts.

"I introduced her to the special room here at Montvale."

Harry sat up straighter in his chair. "My God, Louisa, why? She is a gently born virgin, not a woman who should know about such things..."

Louisa bristled. "Every woman should know about such things, Harry. What on earth makes you think that we should only learn about our bodies from men? What makes you all experts in what gives us pleasure? Should we not know ourselves in order to please ourselves—and our partners? Are you so shallow that a woman with a little sensual knowledge frightens you?"

Harry held up his hand in the classic fencing gesture acknowledging a hit.

"Easy, Louisa. I'm sorry. My choice of words was poor."

Harry grinned as he watched Louisa settle her ruffled feathers, rather like a disturbed broody hen.

He thought briefly of the secret room in Montvale House, which held one of the best collections of sexual toys he'd seen. He also knew that Louisa had a great respect for these toys, and she'd unashamedly told him that she used them regularly. Her firm belief was that an orgasm a day kept her young and vibrant, both spiritually and physically.

If she was anything to go by, then she was absolutely right!

"I merely meant to say that after what she'd been through, the attack and the abuse and so forth, she might not have been in the right frame of mind for such things..." explained Harry patiently.

Louisa humphed.

"Little you know." She smirked at him. "Beatrice took to those toys like she was born and bred to do nothing but enjoy her own body."

Harry's mouth went dry at the thought.

"But there is still an anger there that I can't reach. I didn't realize it until I found her trying to deflower herself with one of the *dilettos*."

Harry gripped the arms of the chair. "You're jesting..."

Louisa shook her head. "No. Sadly not. I stopped her, of course, but the damage had been done, I think. She kept telling me that she would not give that honor to any man. She'd rather an angel took her maidenhead or she'd do it herself, and because she wasn't dead..."

Harry swallowed with difficulty.

"Anyway, I made sure that from that night on, we shared our pleasures together. She now uses her choice of toys regularly and with enthusiasm, but avoids deep penetration, preferring to be stimulated to her peak. I have taught her how to ready her own body. She knows there should be no pain involved."

Harry's breeches were getting tighter by the second as his mind galloped off into a sensual display of images featuring Beatrice naked with a sex toy in her hand, pleasuring herself.

He groaned.

"Agreed, Harry. This situation cannot continue. She must release her anger and find her way back to being the sensual woman she is capable of being."

He stood and walked to the window, lost in thought at the problem before him. He was here at Montvale, not at Louisa's urging, but at the promptings of some inner voice. The same voice that had sneered at all the pussy he'd fucked over the past three months. The same voice that had complained about the taste of each and every woman he'd brought to her peak. The same voice...

Harry sighed. Sometimes inner voices were the bloody end!

"So she needs to release her anger, eh?" he mused, stroking his chin thoughtfully.

"Harry...you do not have to get involved with this if you do not choose to," cautioned Louisa. "Beatrice is a very special woman, and I would rather see her take the veil than be hurt once more."

Harry spun on his heel. "I would never hurt her, Louisa. Never. She's...she's...definitely special."

"To you?"

"That's a very good question." Harry let his words hang in the air, leaving all sorts of unspoken sentiments swirling around them.

"Where is she now?"

"She's gone to spend an hour or so with Mistress Crossley, the old lady who lives in one of the Montvale cottages. She'll be back before dark."

Harry nodded and straightened his spine.

"Very well, Louisa. I have an idea. I'm going to need your help, some of your toys, and then your absence. Will you trust me?"

Louisa looked at Harry, noting the energy that was beginning to churn around him and the sparkle in his eyes. A half-smile played around his sensual lips.

"Of course I trust you, Harry," she answered with complete assurance.

"Good. Here's my plan…"

* * * * *

Beatrice took her time returning to Montvale House from Minerva Crossley's little cottage. The walk was not much more than a mile, but she took advantage of her newly acquired freedom and dawdled along the lane.

The early spring day was lovely, the birds were singing in approval, and all was well with the world. She had heard nothing from her father or indeed any news of Lyndenham, and she was quite content to leave it that way.

This was as close to happiness as she'd ever been. With one exception…

Sighing, Beatrice resolutely dismissed the shiver that crossed her skin at the thought of a pair of dark brown eyes and a mouth that had sent her flying to paradise.

It hadn't been real. Just a figment of her disordered mind. After all, Louisa had told her that she'd given her a small amount of laudanum, and that was known to cause odd visions.

She sighed again. She knew her rescuer had been a friend of Louisa's, but when she'd finally recovered from her ordeal, he'd gone. Louisa had steadfastly refused to divulge his name or where he might live, simply saying that he'd done a good deed and Beatrice should leave it at that.

Beatrice did. But still she was troubled in the nighttime darkness of her room by yearnings for the touch of an angel of desire. Now that she was learning the extent of her own body's response, the feelings of need were becoming more and more unsettling.

She spent sleepless hours recalling how her flesh had hummed at his touch and how the warmth of his tongue had slathered her buttocks. Her nipples would become hard and taut at the simple touch of her nightrobe as it mimicked the rasp of his suckling mouth.

She was becoming accustomed to the juices that ran freely down her thighs as she recalled the heat of his breath on her most secret places. Most nights she had to end this torment herself, sliding her fingers down to her cunt and teasing herself to a teeth-jarring climax. Her angel had awoken the sensual and sexual woman within Beatrice and she was learning to manage it, but it was a constant challenge.

Louisa's toys had certainly helped. A flicker of arousal started low in Beatrice's body as she wondered what Louisa might have in store for them this evening. Their customary routine was dinner, a quiet time with perhaps tea or sherry and their choice of reading material, followed by a bath—sometimes together. Then off to their private domain on an exploration of their sensual selves.

She had developed a preference for the heavy glass pieces. The cool smooth surface slid into her body so easily, stretching, filling, yet so hard that she never mistook them for anything other than what they were.

Nothing could imitate what *he* might feel like, she knew, but such toys were a help.

Louisa had shown her how to prolong the moments before orgasm by simply stopping her movements at just the right point and then resuming her stimulation. Now she was able to tremble on the edge of the precipice for many minutes before making the decision to leap off.

Louisa herself seemed capable of endless hours of arousal, and Beatrice was continually fascinated by the woman's lack of inhibition. Someday soon she thought she might even want to stroke Louisa's soft skin as she was bringing herself pleasure. The image of Louisa as she grew pink and wet and her fingers slid through, over, under and around her own clit had haunted Beatrice for days after the first time they'd shared their pleasure.

Beatrice shook her head at herself, realizing how many scruples she'd shed in the last few months.

But it had been pure fun. Something she'd never experienced before. And the feeling that it was against all she'd been taught was fuel for her rebellious spirit, encouraging her to be as daring as Louisa and try whatever felt good. A laugh caught in her throat and she obeyed an impulse, swirling around in the sunshine. Her little dance brought a flush to her cheeks, and her blonde tresses loosened under her bonnet.

Her steps quickened as she neared the kitchen door. The whinny of a horse caught her attention and she realized that a strange mount had been turned loose to graze in their paddock. They had company?

Beatrice bit her lip. She hoped it might be her savior but was afraid it might be her father. These last weeks had turned her into a woman who could face such an encounter, but she was still not looking forward to it. Well, there was only one way to find out. Squaring her shoulders, she pushed open the gate to the kitchen garden and walked the few steps to the house.

Chapter 6

"Louisa, I'm home…" called Beatrice, as she walked from the kitchen through the passageway to the large foyer of Montvale House.

"In here, Beatrice," answered her friend.

"I saw a horse in the paddock. Do we have company?"

"Sit down, my dear. Have some tea." Louisa poured a steaming cup from the elegant teapot next to her as the two women settled themselves in the small parlor.

"Who's here?" Beatrice was determined to know.

"A gift for you, actually."

"For me?"

"Yes. Something you need that I think you'll also enjoy."

"But why? It is not the Holy Season, and I do not remember my birthday ever being celebrated…"

"Never, my dear?" Louisa's eyes grew round at the thought.

"Never. Having lost my mother at the tender age of four, I have no recollection of whether she may have celebrated the day or not, but for the following twenty years I was required to spend my birthday cleaning the vestry as a way of thanking God for his generosity in allowing me to live."

"Good grief!"

"Yes. I have to admit that I felt rather less than grateful to the Lord upon occasion," said Beatrice wryly.

"This gift is certainly nothing along those lines."

"Very well. Must I guess?" Beatrice folded her hands and lights danced in her blue eyes as she smiled across the tea table.

"No, you must not guess. In fact, you certainly will not guess. But you may hazard a conjecture if you wish," grinned Louisa.

"To judge by your smile, you have procured a new toy for the special room, haven't you?" Beatrice had leaned forward and lowered her voice.

Louisa tilted her head to one side and smiled enigmatically. "I suppose that might well be an appropriate description. Quite accurate, actually."

Beatrice clapped her hands. "There, you see? I outguessed you immediately."

"Well yes and no. Yes, I have procured a new toy, but it's not for the special room—it's for you."

"For me?" squeaked Beatrice.

"You're repeating yourself," smiled Louisa.

"But I...that is, I mean to say, what is there already...um...Louisa...?"

"All will become clear later tonight, my dear. For now, we shall dine and enjoy our usual evening—after your bath, however, you will find a change of clothes that I would ask you to wear."

"This is different, isn't it?" said Beatrice intuitively.

"I hope it will be enjoyable, too."

Beatrice nodded in agreement, feeling a tingle of excitement throbbing low in her belly and a telltale brush of wetness between her thighs. Waiting for tonight would be a challenge to her weakening powers of self-restraint.

* * * * *

The black silk chemise was daring, to say the least!

It barely covered her nipples, which could clearly be seen through the delicate hand-made lace edging the daringly low neckline. It ended at her waist, and it was with a sense of sinful delight that Beatrice had pulled on the matching silk pantaloons.

Scandalous in the extreme, it was rumored that only prostitutes and French women wore such things under their gowns. Beatrice spared a thought for her continental counterparts, shaking her head at the hypocrisy of her countrymen who lumped an entire nation of women together with whores and then made a point of copying their fashions.

She shrugged and turned to the mirror.

She had washed her hair and dried it carefully, combing the tangles away from her face and smoothing it out until it lay like a shawl across her white shoulders. The black silk contrasted sharply with her skin and she could almost catch a glimpse of her short gold curls through the slit in the pantaloons, which offered a teasing glimpse of her pussy when she walked.

It was an erotic ensemble and Beatrice loved it.

A tap on the door was followed by Louisa's entrance.

"Oh good—they do fit," she said, coming over to twitch at Beatrice's straps and make a minor adjustment to the tie of her pantaloons.

Beatrice giggled. "Quite shocking, my dear. Pantaloons!"

"Yes, aren't they lovely? I have some red ones that I find especially pleasant." She ran her hand gently over Beatrice's mound and tickled her clit through the gap in the fabric.

She moaned and moved sensuously against Louisa's fingers. "Louisa—I'm on tenterhooks already. When can I see my surprise?"

"You are not the most patient of women this evening, are you?" grinned Louisa, keeping her touch light and stimulating.

"I have never had a surprise just for me. You know there is no way I can ever thank you or repay you for what you have done for me, Louisa."

Beatrice leaned close and put her arms round Louisa, holding her tightly. Louisa hugged back.

"There is no need, my dear. Your friendship has been a greater gift than any I could bestow." She stroked Beatrice's buttocks gently, knowing the girl was becoming aroused and would be ready now for the night ahead.

Beatrice wriggled under her hands.

"Unless you want to stay here and have us reach our peaks together tonight in this room, you'd better stop that." Beatrice pressed her bottom into Louisa's hands, feeling safe, warm, and loved.

Louisa sighed.

"Come along then," she answered.

Beatrice was practically skipping on tiptoes through the silent and deserted master suite to the bookshelves that skillfully concealed the door to so many sexual mysteries.

The door had been left ajar, and she could tell that a good-sized fire was burning and that the candles had been lit.

She stepped inside and froze.

There was a naked man hanging from the ceiling!

* * * * *

Harry tensed as he heard the indrawn breath from near the door. He could only imagine what kind of picture he presented.

He'd stripped and bathed, and used the oil of sandalwood that Louisa had given him. He knew his body gleamed in the firelight and was fairly certain that he had nothing to be ashamed of. He'd never shirked any kind of physical activity, and although he was not far off his thirty-eighth year, he still possessed a well-muscled chest and little if any extra flesh around his waist. His bed partners had invariably complimented his backside and years of riding good horseflesh had given him rock-solid thighs.

His hands were fastened with manacles and hooked over a bar, which Louisa had lowered from the high ceiling. One good twist and he'd be free, but there was no reason for Beatrice to know that interesting fact.

Nor did she need to know that the hood covering his head was not as opaque as it looked. The black silk over his eyes was so sheer that he could see Beatrice clearly as she neared him with mouth agape.

"Louisa..." The voice was hers, low and soft, and it did things to Harry's cock. Nice things. "What is this?"

"This, my dear Beatrice, is a man."

"I can see that," she murmured, eyeing his cock with interest as she circled him, but staying cautiously away from his body. "What am I supposed to do with him?"

"Anything you wish."

"Anything?"

"Anything."

"Ah." Harry noted Beatrice licking her lips. His gut tightened.

Louisa rattled her keys and a door to a low cabinet opened, drawing Beatrice's eyes away from the sight of his erection, which apparently fascinated her.

"If I may suggest," Louisa reached into the cabinet, and both Harry and Beatrice watched as she withdrew several items.

"Beatrice, it is time for you to lay your anger to rest. You have been hurt and mistreated through no fault of your own, but you will be the one punished unless you free yourself of these mental chains." She offered a flat piece of wood to Beatrice by the handle.

"Here is your chance to exorcise your demons. Punish the man who hurt you, punish the man who never loved you the way a father should. Beat the blazes out of every man who ever raised his hand to a woman."

Louisa moved behind Harry and he braced himself.

A sharp slap of her naked hand across his buttocks rang through the room. It did not hurt, merely tingled. Harry's cock, however, paid close attention.

Beatrice was looking doubtful.

"I don't know, Louisa..."

"I do. This man will not hurt you, he has offered to do this for your pleasure."

Beatrice raised her eyes and looked at his hooded face for the first time, as if remembering that he was, in fact, real.

"Is this true, sir?"

Harry nodded, keeping silent lest she recognize his voice.

Louisa slipped from the room and closed the door behind her, the click of the lock sounding like a cannon in the stillness.

The two people surveyed each other, Harry noting the vivid flush that was spreading across Beatrice's white skin and her nipples that were beading and pushing hard against the lace of her chemise. Her breasts rose and fell rapidly, and she again licked her lips.

She moved behind Harry.

"Well, sir, it seems you are to pay for the sins of your sex," she murmured, weighing the paddle in her hand. "But I dislike this tool, let me see..."

Harry could hear rummaging going on but could not see what she was doing. To move and look would give away the fact that he had some vision from behind his hood.

"Now this might do the trick." He jumped as a leather thong landed squarely across his backside.

"Oh, I'm sorry, did that hurt? Here, let me try this..." Beatrice's voice was apologetic and Harry shuddered as he felt a softness caress his tingling flesh. It was furry and Beatrice was rubbing it lovingly over and around his buttocks.

Beneath the mask he closed his eyes.

"It is a fox tail, I believe," she murmured, more to herself than him. "But it will not achieve the goal Louisa believes I must accomplish, will it?"

She removed the tail from his flesh and another stinging lash landed. He flinched.

"I'm sorry...this must be so painful," said Beatrice, her voice shaking.

"Continue," growled Harry, making his voice harsh and low. "Please continue."

"Are you sure?"

No. "Yes." He nodded to signify his desire so that she would understand clearly. He also silently screamed at his body to get control of itself.

"Very well..."

Several strokes followed, none hard, but each sounding solid. Harry's buttocks were burning now, and his cock and his balls were approaching the same state. He'd not been a visitor to the many Punishment Parlors that were rife in London's sexual underworld, but perhaps he'd been missing something.

Or perhaps it was just this fairy in black silk that aroused him to such a pitch.

A brush with the fox's tail brought a drop of moisture to his cock.

Beatrice warmed to her task.

"This is for my father," she said, lashing him hard. "And for the curate..." Another solid shot cracked across him. "And for women who never had this chance..."

A final slashing blow brought a hiss to Harry's lips and he couldn't hide the shudder of pain or the sweat that was rolling freely down his chest.

"Oh, God, I cannot..." Beatrice ran around in front of him and threw the flogger across the room. "I have hurt you, how could I do that? I am no better than they..."

She reached for his shackles, unaware that her body was pressed tight to his from breast to thigh. How she ignored the cock that was threatening to impale her he had no idea.

She could barely manage, and as she rubbed herself against him trying to unclasp his manacles, he lost all semblance of control.

One twist and he was free.

One more twist and his hood fell to the floor.

"You!"

"Yes, my angel, it's me."

Chapter 7

Beatrice stood as still as a statue while Harry freed himself from the manacles and dropped them to his feet.

"I thought you were a dream," she whispered, raising one hand as if to touch him, then pausing.

Harry grabbed her hand and brought it solidly to his chest.

"No dream, Beatrice, I'm real. I'm here. Feel me, run your hands over me. God, I've wanted this ever since you first looked at me and called me beautiful."

Beatrice inched closer and leaned her breasts against him, running her hands over his face and shoulders as she gazed at him.

"You held me, and saved me, and you touched me…" She blushed as she remembered and her eyes darkened.

Harry felt his control slipping even further as he slid his hands around her body, cupping her buttocks.

She gasped as he lifted her and tucked his cock into the notch of her thighs. His movements parted the silk of her pantaloons and she felt his hardness rubbing against her swollen flesh. Her juices flowed freely, wetting the silk and his cock.

"Beatrice, let me show you all there is…" Harry's lips grazed hers. "Let me finish the lessons we began last winter." His fingers clenched her buttocks, spreading them apart slightly. "Let me love you until you can't even remember your own name…"

"Oh, God, please…" she begged, wriggling in his arms and trying to get even closer.

Harry stepped over to the odd Oriental couch, which had clearly been designed with passion in mind. He lowered his burden gently to its soft surface, noting how nicely her head nestled on the one arm, and how well he'd fit between her thighs. One leg sprawled off the side of the couch and the lack of an arm on the other end would facilitate what was to come. Clever folks, these Orientals.

He settled himself right where he wanted to be, keeping most of his weight on his arms.

He smiled at her.

She smiled back.

He gripped her chemise with his teeth and pulled, grinning around a mouthful of silk at the ripping sound.

Beatrice gasped as he spat out the silk and lowered his head to her breasts.

He tugged and pulled and swirled with his tongue, always aware of Beatrice's response. He smiled around her nipple as her little sighs and moans told him of her pleasure in his actions.

He gently slid a hand to her waist and slipped the tie of her pantaloons free, spreading the silk away from her pussy. Her fragrance filled his nostrils and his soul, making him as dizzy as he was aroused.

Beatrice was now thrusting her hips against him. Hot, wet and ready, she let him know in no uncertain terms that she needed him. Now.

"Beatrice, love, are you sure?" He stroked her curls and flicked her clit with his fingers, eliciting a groan of frustration from the angel beneath him. He slid the pantaloons away from her body, freeing her completely to his gaze.

A very unholy growl emerged. "*Now*, for God's sake, before I explode!"

Stifling his triumphant grin, Harry lifted his body slightly and grasped his cock, settling it amidst the hot and swollen flesh between her thighs.

"Beatrice, look at me…"

She opened her eyes, and tried to focus through her haze of passion.

"I want to watch your face as I make you come…"

He gently moved his hips forward, sliding blissfully into her cunt with nary a check to bar his way.

Her eyes grew large as she realized she held him within her.

"Are you really inside me?"

"Indeed I am," gritted out Harry. "See for yourself…"

He pulled back out and gestured with his head for her to look.

Beatrice raised herself up on one elbow and stared at the sight of Harry's swollen cock covered with her juices as it slid in and out of her body.

He pushed all the way in until his balls touched her skin and their pubic hair tangled. They looked at each other and gently Harry leaned forward and placed a tender kiss on her parted lips.

It was a moment of magic that seemed to release the need within Beatrice. Her hips thrust against his and her hands were suddenly everywhere.

Harry met her need with thrusts of his own, deeper and stronger, the sounds of their bodies meeting in this heated fucking simply adding to their frenzy.

Beatrice moaned as he slid his fingers between their bodies and over her clit. She was hotter than fire around his cock, and he knew he was within seconds of surrendering. Her fingers traced the cleft of his buttocks and delved between as she hung on to his pounding hips.

Her cries were getting louder, and his movements faster and tighter.

Neither could last.

With one last mighty grunt, Harry exploded inside her, the feel of his come spurting warmly against her womb pushing Beatrice into meeting his orgasm with her own.

Harry held himself rigid, feeling his cock being drained by the incredible spasms inside her body. Her thighs clamped his with iron strength, her fingernails were leaving marks on his back and her face was taut with her release.

His mind blanked out, his heart soared, and he knew he'd never be the same.

* * * * *

Many hours later, a firm knock on the doorjamb heralded the arrival of Louisa into the room.

Groggily, Harry and Beatrice untangled themselves, and Harry pulled a soft shawl over Beatrice's body.

"Well, I see that all is as it should be," smiled Louisa.

Two remarkably similar grins answered her.

"And no more talk of a convent, Miss Beatrice?"

"Definitely not," she smiled, unable to resist touching Harry's shoulder.

They'd spent the entire night exploring each other, loving each other, and finding new and exciting places to lick and kiss and fondle. They'd shared orgasms, brought each other to their peaks with their hands and their tongues, played with the odd toy, and were completely sated in the aftermath of such pleasure.

Harry just lay there and smiled like an idiot, loving the touch of his Beatrice's fingers. Anywhere. But probably not *there*, especially not with Louisa in the room. He caught up the small hand in his before it strayed too far, and squeezed it lovingly.

Louisa ignored the sexual play and threw back the curtains from the small windows. "It is morning, my friends, and time for some decisions. A message arrived at first light. Your father has learned of your presence here, Beatrice. He is on his way."

Beatrice's body tensed, but Harry was right there holding and soothing her.

"We shall take care of him once and for all, my love." He dropped a kiss on her nose. "Do not forget you agreed to wed me, somewhere around dawn, and as your affianced husband, I am well within my rights to take care of this matter on your behalf."

Beatrice relaxed and blushed as she remembered *exactly* what she'd been doing when he had asked her to marry him. She'd had to nod her reply because she'd had her mouth full at the time. She cleared her throat.

"Very well, my heart. I do have one question, though…"

"What's that, sweet?"

"What's your name?"

* * * * *

"The Earl of Dunsmere," intoned the butler loudly.

A very elegant gentleman entered the room where the Vicar of Lyndenham was furiously pacing a rut into the carpet.

"What…what is this? I demand to see my daughter…"

Raising his quizzing glass to his eye, the Earl silently surveyed Reverend Shelton from boots to receding hairline.

Harsh lines marred his cheeks, his clothes were rank and dusty, and his eyes cold. Inside, Harry shuddered.

"Your daughter, sir?" he inquired languidly.

"Beatrice, that hell-spawned bitch. Probably ran away with some whoreson and spread her legs for whatever she could get," he spat.

It was with great satisfaction that Harry, Earl of Dunsmere, punched the Vicar of Lyndenham right in the nose and knocked him flat on the floor.

"Is he dead?" asked Beatrice from the doorway.

"'Fraid not," answered Harry, rubbing his knuckles. "He's got a harder head than that."

The Reverend sputtered as he saw Beatrice watching him with a distasteful look on her face. The fact that she wore an elegant gown was obviously not lost on her father.

"Just as I thought. You've been whoring your way into decent people's homes, you...you daughter of Satan." He wiped the blood away from his lip with a skinny hand.

Harry kicked him in the ribs before he could get up. Rather unsporting, but enormously satisfying.

Beatrice applauded.

Louisa, standing behind Beatrice, heaved a sigh of relief and watched as Harry leaned over the recumbent reverend.

"You, sir, are being disrespectful to the future Countess of Dunsmere. *I* don't like it. Neither does she."

The Reverend's mouth fell open.

"Should you even mention her name again, I shall hear about it. And so will Lord Lynden, a good friend of mine. He holds your living, I believe..."

The man's face had turned pasty white and he scrambled cautiously to his feet.

"I didn't mean, that is...I didn't know..." he stuttered.

"Get out of my sight. If my wife or I ever see your face or hear from you again, the only congregation you'll be tending will be a flock of sheep on the remotest Scottish island I can find. Do I make myself clear?"

The Reverend attempted a bow and failed miserably. He scurried from the room a broken man, not even glancing at his daughter as he left.

Beatrice and Louisa moved aside, Beatrice pulling her skirts back as if to avoid contamination.

She went straight into Harry's arms as soon as the door closed behind her father.

"Thank you, Harry," she smiled, hugging every bit of him she could get her arms around.

Louisa left the room silently, eyes meeting Harry's over Beatrice's head. The look they exchanged spoke of warmth and love, and thanks from Harry for the miracle he was now holding.

"It was my pleasure, sweetheart. Actually, now that I come to think of it, your pleasure is my pleasure too. And I can't remember how long ago it was that I gave you your pleasure..."

"Oh, ages and ages. At least an hour," whispered his love, as his hands slid her silky dress up her thighs.

"I think I shall be happy spending the rest of my life doing this, my heart. Touching you, learning you, loving you..."

His fingers found that for which he sought.

"And of course, there's this too..."

"And what might that be, my soon-to-be-husband?" grinned Beatrice, wriggling herself further into his arms.

Harry closed his eyes and hummed his pleasure as his hands caressed and squeezed the softness he'd discovered.

"Why the ultimate prize, of course...my Beatrice's bottom!"

Epilogue

The Earl of Dunsmere squirmed in his bathtub as the Countess of Dunsmere tucked her toes in around his balls and wiggled them.

"Oh, God, Beatrice," he sighed.

Beatrice giggled.

The servants at the London residence of the Earl and Countess had quickly become used to the rather sybaritic behavior on the part of their master and his new bride. Bets were actually being placed upon the number of times each day the couple would find an excuse to lock the door, take a bath, retire to their rooms, or otherwise manage to be quite alone.

So far the biggest winner had been the second scullery maid who had bet on seven for the previous Wednesday. It was the highest she could count. She'd been smiling ever since, but no more so than the Earl and his loving wife.

Who was now rendering delightful physical torture on her husband's balls.

"We can't stay for too long, Harry. Lord and Lady Barbour will be arriving soon," reminded Beatrice.

Harry ran gentle fingers up his wife's thigh.

"Nick, of all people, will forgive us if we're late."

"I hear Lady Miranda is with child..."

"So Nick says. Hard to believe that hellion is going to be a father." His fingers moved on, bringing a shiver to his wife's skin.

"Do you want children, Harry?"

He paused and considered the matter. "Yes."

"Good."

Harry glanced at his wife's flushed countenance and then noticed her breasts, swollen and ready for his mouth. They seemed a little larger than normal.

"Beatrice...are you saying..." he nearly choked trying to get the words out.

Beatrice smiled tentatively at him and nodded.

His leap for his wife sloshed most of the water out of the tub, which would aggravate his housekeeper to no end.

He didn't care. Harry Boyd just wanted to get his arms around his wife...and their child.

Meanwhile, in Yorkshire all was quiet, and Louisa felt strangely unsettled. The rooms seemed empty and her toys held no appeal. She didn't know that within a few moments there would be an explosion in a small London laboratory that would send shockwaves all the way to Montvale House—and perhaps into her very soul...

THE END

LYING WITH LOUISA

Chapter 1

The man in the bed moaned.

It was a slight sound, but it was enough to awaken Louisa Cellini from her doze in the chair near the fire.

She stretched her arms above her head as she stood, letting the wool blanket that had been covering her fall to the floor.. Her nude body gleamed in the flickering firelight, and she bent to add another log. Satisfied that the wood had caught, she turned to the bed.

He was tossing and moving his head back and forth on the pillow, his over-long sandy colored hair tangling and matting beneath him.

Louisa eased her hip onto the bed next to him and reached for the cloths soaking in cool water. She gently placed one across his forehead and his fidgeting immediately stilled.

He sighed, as if in relief.

Louisa gently ran her fingers down his beard-stubbled cheek, soothing as much as caressing.

His arm moved out towards her and when it touched her thigh, he turned his whole body, swinging his other arm over her leg and holding on to her.

She adjusted the cool cloth and continued her gentle stroking, over his shoulders, down his forearms, and back to his hair which she carefully smoothed free of knots.

And still he slept.

Louisa found her stroking was having a hypnotic effect on her as well, and she gazed at the man lying next to her with a mixture of emotions.

He was an inventor. A man with a brilliant and inquisitive mind, or so she'd been told. A man who also possessed a body that was mouthwateringly attractive, and designed to catch a woman's eye. Most especially her eyes, which traveled down his muscled length, enjoying the sight of his firm flesh, and his perfectly proportioned manhood lying relaxed amongst sandy curls.

She could enjoy the sight, but it was marred by the shining wound that crossed from one ankle to corrupt the skin of his calf then traveled on up towards his outer leg. One hand was bandaged, the one that was lying so casually across her thigh.

But Louisa knew the worst wound was not revealed by puckered flesh or clean white bandages. It was the one that he had suffered when his equipment had blown up in front of him.

The astounding flash of light that had singed his eyebrows, splattered him with flaming chemicals—and stolen his sight.

Professor Owen Lloyd-Jones was blind.

* * * * *

He settled himself more comfortably next to Louisa, and his breath warmed her thigh as she watched him.

It had been two days since his arrival, which had been heralded by a rider from London with a message from the Countess of Dunsmere.

Recognizing her friend Beatrice's handwriting, Louisa had slit the envelope open with a smile, only to be intrigued by the message within.

"Louisa my dearest,

Harry and I are sending you a special patient who needs all your skill and attention. We cannot think of another who might help him find his way out of the darkness. Please, Louisa, he needs you very badly."

Within hours the Earl's traveling carriage had pulled up at Montvale House and disgorged its single passenger, the mostly unconscious and injured Professor Owen Lloyd-Jones. The papers tucked into his jacket told the story.

He'd been working in his laboratory when an experiment had gone drastically wrong. The details about magnesium, elements, something called electricity, and vapors, went by Louisa's mind like water over a waterfall. They didn't matter to her.

What did matter was the magnificent man who had been burned by his experiments and robbed of his sight. His eyebrows would grow back to their full bushy state, but his eyes...

The physician's note had been hopeful. He could not, he said, presently detect any permanent damage to the Professor's eyes. He cited a similar tragedy, which had befallen noted investigator Sir Humphry Davy some years before. A malfunctioning experiment had rendered him temporarily blind, but his sight had returned within weeks.

Louisa had rushed to the carriage and found Owen, still drugged with the laudanum that had helped ease his pain. His pupils were so dilated that his eyes seemed black as he stared at nothing.

She had taken his hand in hers and led him to her room, undressing him carefully and laying him between her sheets. His body had called to hers as she cleaned and tended to his wounds, yet he had remained silent. His cock had become aroused as she'd washed him, and she'd been unable to refrain from gently stroking it. Then he'd moaned, and she'd remembered what she was supposed to be doing.

Honey had been substituted for the heavy wrappings on his leg, light cotton now covered the scrapes on his hand, and her own mixture of valerian and herbs was replacing the drugging laudanum. His body was already showing signs of recovery.

All that was left was his eyes.

He must be around forty, thought Louisa, as she settled herself more comfortably on the bed next to him. His hand slipped from her thigh onto the bed, and she found herself missing its warmth.

His body was very nicely sculpted, firm and masculine. His shoulders were broad and his skin was golden. He must have done a lot of research outdoors without a shirt, she mused.

His waist was trim, his chest downy with hair, and his belly lean and flat. He struck her as a man who moved a lot, there was banked energy stored in those muscles. His thighs would be strong and firm and she found herself yearning for their feel between her legs.

She wriggled a little as her speculations aroused her. Slipping her hand to her mound, she felt the moisture pooling and flowing from her hungry flesh. As one who enjoyed a healthful daily orgasm, Louisa knew all there was to know about pleasuring herself.

So why was she responding to the mere presence of this man? What was it about him that made her hot and wet? She could not recall ever becoming this aroused by a male, they were basically unnecessary to her pleasure. And Louisa did believe in her own pleasure, just not in needing a man to achieve it.

She could have fetched one of her favorite toys from her private playroom and used it to relieve her needs, but tonight she was next to a special person—she wanted to savor the moment.

She raised her knee, and his uninjured hand slipped beneath her thigh. A mere slide of her hips and his hand would be on her mound. She found herself powerless to resist.

Her hand closed over his long fingers and guided them to her aching flesh. Spreading her thighs, she touched his hand to her clit.

It was as if one of his experiments had come to life. There was a vibrant tingle where his warmth caressed hers, and when she pressed him deep against her folds, her body started shuddering.

She rubbed herself gently at first, not wanting to disturb him, but needing the contact.

With her free hand, she cupped her breasts, lifting, pulling, and finally pinching her nipples.

Her head dropped back and she ground his fingers into her sensitive tissues as her buttocks clenched and her juices flowed over his hand.

She teased her nipples, first one and then the other, the dart of sensation adding to the building tension within her.

His fingers were just the right shape to cover her mound, and she moved so that she could hold him even tighter against her. She wanted him inside her so badly she could taste it, but didn't dare push his hand any deeper.

Patiently she masturbated against his hand, allowing the texture of his skin to imprint itself on her slick flesh. The sensations built and her mouth opened in a silent gasp as she neared her orgasm.

His hand stiffened and suddenly there were three long, firm fingers inside her. Unquestioningly she welcomed them, their warmth and vitality spreading ripples of sensation through her shaking body. The shock and the feeling of fullness completed her spiral into ecstasy.

The orgasm shook her to her core.

As rational thought returned, she noticed his hand was gone. Turning, she looked at her patient.

He still slept, but she could have sworn there was a slight curve to his lips.

Chapter 2

He could smell her on his fingers.

His mind was still foggy, his thoughts rambling hither and yon, but he had the smell of a woman on his fingers and the remembered feel of her hot and silky cunt in his mind. He would have dismissed it as a dream but for that fragrance.

He stretched slightly, feeling the tug of injured skin halting his movements. Oh yes — the laboratory. The electrical current had been unstable and overcharged through the magnesium sample he'd been using.

His body tightened as the details of the explosion began to filter through his returning consciousness. There'd been a sudden whirr of his homemade electrical system and a hiss within the Leyden jar that held the capacitor. His mind recalled a loud sound and a bright light — then nothing.

He'd been injured, that much was certain.

There were vague memories of voices, shouting at first, then soothing. There were moments when he could have sworn he was in a carriage, but there were other moments of complete emptiness.

He had no idea where he was, but he felt comfortable at least. The room he was in was warm, the sheets soft and smelled of lavender and sunshine. It was quiet, and some sense told him that he was, for the moment, alone.

And of course, there was her.

The woman whose scent lingered on his skin and his pillows. He had heard her voice through his confusion, low and soft, with a touch of an accent now and again.

He had felt her hand soothing his naked body, even stroking his cock as she tended to him. In his drugged state he'd acknowledged the touch but had been helpless to do anything about it.

And then he'd woken to find her close to him, her warmth around him and her most sensitive folds under his fingers.

It had to have been one of the most erotic moments he could remember, although heaven knew there hadn't been many erotic moments in his life up to now. He was powerless to resist the urge to drive his fingers into her soaking cunt and explore her deepest secrets.

Of course he'd had women. Every man had the need for an occasional release. But the women who had pursued him in his youth had given up when they realized that his true mistress was science. They couldn't hope to fight the lure of the base metals or the pipette, the excitement of the moments before an experiment worked, or the incredible, almost sexual thrill of a successful invention.

Most of the time, he'd taken matters into his own hands and brought himself to orgasm as the need overtook him. And recently that had been less and less. He was going to be forty-two this year and his sexual inclinations were obviously waning.

So how to explain the fact that the scent of this woman on his hand and the memory of his fingers up her cunt were giving him a magnificent erection?

He eased himself onto his back, cataloging his sensations. A pulling tightness on the outside of one leg. One hand was bandaged, but the other was free. The one that had been in *her*.

His cock hardened even more at the recollection. It was becoming painful in its arousal and Owen knew he'd get no rest until he'd relieved the problem.

He listened intently to the stillness within the room with eyes closed, feigning sleep. Hearing nothing, he lowered his uninjured hand to his groin and grasped his cock firmly, wishing that he could be buried in something softer, hotter and wetter.

He stroked with decisive movements, lingering for mere seconds at the ridge and head, but adding a quick flick to the small slit as drops of moisture began to bead their way across its swollen surface. His whole mind was focused on his cock and the sensations that were building there.

His balls tightened and he felt a tingle at the base of his spine. He moved his hand faster now, wanting to prolong the exquisite anticipation, but finding that his body was rushing headlong into the vortex.

With an indrawn breath his climax was upon him, and his hand pumped furiously as he came.

His seed spurted joyfully from his cock and his clamped muscles unwound, easing him into a state of exhausted relaxation.

Sighing, he opened his eyes. His body jerked once in disbelief.

He was quite blind.

Owen raised a hand to his eyes, touching the skin around them gently. He passed trembling fingers over the stubble of his eyebrows and then covered them completely.

His body heaved with a sob.

"You are not alone." A voice swept through the blackness surrounding him. "I am here, Owen. You are not alone."

Owen froze. Especially when a soft hand touched his abdomen and smoothed his cum around like lotion below his navel.

"Who are you?" he asked roughly, a trace of embarrassment in his voice.

"A friend."

"Where am I?"

"You are in my home."

"Answers but no answers. Are you some kind of Sibyl? A wise woman who is supposed to tend to me? Take me by the hand for the rest of my life? Hold my cock when I need to empty my bladder? God, woman, *I CAN'T SEE!*"

Louisa flinched at the deep and abiding pain that flowed from his heart to his words and into her soul.

"I know." She continued to smooth her hand over his flesh, dipping down around his cock and his balls now and again.

"So who are you, besides my 'friend'?"

Louisa sighed. She could hear the anger begin. It was good, a natural progression. Better anger than desperation.

"I am Louisa Cellini. You are presently in my room at Montvale House in Yorkshire."

"Yorkshire? How did I get here?"

"After the explosion in your laboratory, Harry Boyd arranged for you to come here to recuperate. He and I have been friends for years."

"So, one of Harry's women. That explains it."

Louisa removed her hand. "Explains what?"

"Are you a simple whore, or were you Harry's mistress? I hope he's paying you well for looking after a blind man like this."

Louisa began to clean his skin with a warm cloth, washing him gently but thoroughly. His anger was clearly directed at her, but she knew that whoever had been here at this time would have been a convenient target.

"I am not a whore. I am a friend of Harry's, *and* his wife's, and have been for many years. I am tending to you because he asked it of me and for no other reason. Certainly not for financial gain. This is my home, I have no need of anyone's support."

Her voice remained calm in spite of the insults Owen flung at her.

"No decent woman would behave as you do. How long have you been here at my bedside? Did you enjoy watching me come? Why didn't you say something? Another woman would have immediately made her presence known."

Louisa was silent for a moment as she dried him off. "I have been here for some time, and yes, I enjoyed watching you come. You have a beautiful body and your face is very lovely and full of passion when you spend your seed. I believe that there is nothing wrong with being aware of one's sexual and sensual needs. I enjoy an orgasm every day, and feel the better for it. Does that make me indecent?"

Owen chewed his lip. "I don't know. It makes you different. If I could look into your eyes, I might be able to tell. But I shall be denied that pleasure, shan't I?"

The bitterness was unmistakable, and Louisa responded to it.

"The damage may not be permanent, Owen. The physician could find no obvious sign of damage. He is encouraged that, given time, you will regain your sight."

"And until then? I'm a worthless cripple. I can walk, talk, and do everything a healthy man can do, but I cannot see to do it. I'm a scientist, an investigator, Madam. I rely on my eyes to function. Now I will have to be led around like a sick animal. Perhaps it would have been better if I'd died in that explosion. Better to be in heaven than in this dark hell."

Louisa gently pulled the covers over him.

"Why are you caring for me?" he asked, flinging his arm across his eyes. "Why waste your time with half a man? You're a woman who admits to enjoying her body. Why aren't you fucking your husband?"

"I have no husband, Owen. No man owns or controls me, nor will there ever be such a man. The pleasure I enjoy I give myself. It's easier that way. And I do not accept that you are only half a man, either."

She raised him slightly and held a cup to his lips.

"Drink, Owen, 'tis a harmless blend of herbs that will ease your mind and help you rest. At the moment, rest is the best medicine in the world. Your burns are healing well and your hand is improving daily. It is time to call upon that scientific patience for which you are renowned. Imagine this is an experiment..."

She eased him back on the pillows and tugged his arm away from his face. Soothing his brow with her hand, she softened her voice even more.

"You are a famous and brilliant scientist, and now you must wait to see the results of this experiment. After a while you will be able to tell if it has been a success, but you must not expect too much too soon."

Owen's breathing slowed slightly. "But I'm blind, Louisa. I can't see you. I can't see anything. I shall not be able to live like this. I shall never feel..."

His voice tapered off as the herbal tincture took effect.

"Not feel, eh? We shall have to see about that, my very handsome friend, we shall have to see..."

Chapter 3

For the next few days Louisa deliberately stayed away from Owen's sickroom. Her servants were efficient and well trained, and took excellent care of him, withstanding his verbal assaults and his demands that Louisa present herself.

She was encouraged by his temper tantrums. The lingering effects of the laudanum had worn off, and the burned skin was healing extremely well. Only his sight was still affected. He was unable to see anything at all.

His frustration was growing as his strength returned, and Louisa knew she could not keep him in bed much longer. The time was drawing near to start educating Professor Lloyd-Jones on what the rest of his body could do, even though his eyes weren't working.

Louisa licked her lips. Her plan to provide a distraction for Owen was likely to provide a distraction for her as well. Each night since he'd staggered into her life she'd found her pleasure, but somehow now her sexual playthings were bringing her less and less satisfaction.

Only the night before, she'd been in her special room, naked before the fire with her favorite wooden *diletto* in her hand.

This room had been her sanctuary for many years and its contents had brought her much pleasure, not to mention teaching her and her special friends a great deal about their bodies and their capability for sexual satisfaction. It was entirely possible that both Harry Boyd and his friend, Lord Nicholas Barbour, were enjoying happy marriages because of this room.

Their wives had been able students of the erotic lessons offered by these antiques.

But this night, Louisa had found to her surprise that she'd ended up fantasizing about Owen's hand between her legs instead of a wooden phallus. She'd had no difficulty imagining his tongue caressing her taut nipples or her eager clit.

She'd not needed the toy — it had dropped from her hands as she touched herself. With eyes closed, she'd seen his strong face above her, felt his weight crushing into her and enjoyed his touch on her clit. Her nipples had seemed more sensitive than usual as she caressed them and pinched them, using the near-painful sensation to heighten her arousal. She'd imagined his mouth suckling her breasts, licking, nibbling, and pleasuring both of them. She'd felt his touch on the fragile skin of her belly and imagined his weight holding her thighs down as he thrust into her. He'd be firm and strong and he'd be able to plunge deep into her innermost secrets.

Yearning, she'd writhed alone, plunging her fingers into her cunt and knowing that it wasn't the same. She was forty-four years old, and suddenly she wanted a man. Not just any man, but the one lying in her bed.

The orgasm she'd experienced had been one of amazing strength. Truly, the presence of Owen Lloyd-Jones was proving to be quite a disturbance for her. It was time to put his feet on the road to recovery.

Louisa felt her thighs tighten and her juices flow at the thought. Tonight she would begin Owen's reintroduction to his body. She was going to awaken his sensuality. Show him that there were some things for which sight was unnecessary. And she had a feeling he was going to be *very* good at them.

She allowed herself a little grin.

* * * * *

Owen heard the door open and close, and knew it was *her*.

"So, you've finally decided to visit the blind man, have you?" he snarled angrily.

"Yes."

"About time."

"Haven't my servants been taking good care of you?"

"You know they have. I'm sure they report every scab and wrinkle in my skin, not to mention the number of times they have to help me use the chamber pot."

Louisa chuckled. "Not quite that detailed a report, Owen. But I'm glad that they have shaved you. At least now I can see the man beneath the stubble..."

Owen touched his hand to his smooth cheek, unwilling to admit that he felt a lot better without his half-grown beard.

"So why are you here? I still can't see, you know," he said, flinging himself petulantly back against the pillows.

"But it appears that you have your temper back, and I thought you might like to get up and move around a little this evening."

Owen cringed at the thought. "I suppose you'll take me by the hand, and pick me up when I trip over the furniture?" he replied sarcastically.

"Do you like sex, Owen?"

Good god. Where had that come from? He wasn't sure how to respond. "Er—well..."

"How silly of me," continued Louisa in her calm voice. "Of course you do. At least with yourself."

Owen couldn't help the blush that crept over his newly smoothed cheeks. "I cannot believe you would mention that episode," he said.

"Why not? You have a beautiful body. It was a pleasure to watch you."

"You are a sexually obsessed woman, Miss Cellini. It cannot be healthful," pronounced Owen at his most pedantic.

"Bosh! I am forty-four years old and I know how to pleasure myself. I am not ashamed of it. I have not suffered anything more than a touch of the ague in many years, and I still ride, walk, and have all my teeth. I run this estate profitably, and my neighbors are mostly pleasant and don't hesitate to visit. I enjoy my own touch, rather than a man's, because I have not yet found a man willing to consider my pleasure as well as his. Nor am I looking for one. If this is wrong, please enlighten me."

Owen was at a loss as to how to reply to Louisa's blunt speech. His cock, however, clearly heard something that fascinated it, as Owen could feel his erection beginning. Damned if she wasn't seducing him with her words.

"I feel differently about you and your body, Owen, than I have felt for any man before." Owen knew Louisa was moving around the room as she spoke, he could hear her gown rustling.

"Perhaps this is because you cannot see me, or judge *my* body. As I said, I am forty-four. No longer are my breasts high and tight, nor is my skin unlined. The passage of time has marked me as surely as the explosion has marked you. I would like for us to turn this situation to our mutual advantage."

"And how do you suggest we do that?" inquired Owen, not sure if he wanted to hear the answer, but feeling a warmth in his loins.

"Firstly, this…" Louisa had come close to him and he felt the soft touch of silk across his face.

"What…what…" he sputtered as she tied a piece of fabric over his eyes.

"In many sexual experiences, one partner is blindfolded. For this evening, we are going to pretend that you cannot see because you are thus arrayed." She tightened the knot behind his head.

Owen was silent as he realized that she had changed his perspective slightly. Feeling the silk tight against his closed eyes made his blindness seem like his choice, not his fate. A small difference, but a difference all the same.

"Now, you will leave the bed, yes?"

Feeling her hand tugging his, Owen carefully slid his legs towards her, sensing the edge of the bed and easing himself upright. He realized, rather belatedly, that he was stark naked.

"I...um...a robe, perhaps?"

"Oh I think not," came a low chuckle from his side. "But if you are uncomfortable, perhaps this will put your mind at rest."

He felt her touch on his hand as she raised it and brought it to—where? Owen focused and let his mind see what his eyes could not. She was using his hand to brush something soft away from her body. She lowered his hand and together their fingers tugged on a cord. He heard the 'swoosh' of material as her garment fell to the floor.

"I am naked too, Owen. Feel me."

She ran his hand from her waist up over her breast to her neck. It was the most exquisite sensation, and Owen's cock agreed. Strongly.

"You said you would not be able to feel anything, Owen. This night will prove you wrong," purred Louisa.

She released his hand, leaving him bereft.

"Follow my voice, Owen. Come to me. Take three, maybe four, steps forward. There is no furniture between us..."

Hesitantly, Owen took a shaky step forward. Nothing barred his way.

"That's right, come to me, my fine gentleman."

Another step and he was closer still. It was almost as if he could feel the warmth of her flesh calling to him.

A final step and his cock bumped something soft.

"You have reached me," said Louisa unnecessarily. "Can you feel me?"

"Of course, woman," snorted Owen. "My cock is stabbing you. What do you think I feel?"

"I do not know. You are the one who said he couldn't feel."

Owen had a sneaking suspicion that he might well regret using those exact words.

She moved away.

Owen sucked in his breath.

"Relax and tell me if you like this..."

She was behind him, and something soft, two somethings actually, were caressing his buttocks. Two somethings with little nubs. Little hard nubs. Good god, she was rubbing her breasts over his backside.

He groaned.

"Oh, we can feel that, can we?"

His cock answered for him, producing a small tear of joy.

Her hands reached around him and stroked the drop gently down his length.

He moaned.

"That too, I hear."

Owen gritted his teeth. "Very well. I can achieve an arousal. You can probably make me come as well. But whether I shall truly feel it without being able to watch you as it happens is the question, isn't it?"

He felt rather than heard Louisa's low laugh.

"Oh, I think we can answer that question, my friend. Take my hand." She led him carefully to what felt like the soft back of a sofa.

"Bend over."

* * * * *

Louisa was surprised by the fact that Owen did as she told him without demur. It was a mark of how much trust he had developed over the past days.

"Well, what now?" he asked impatiently, forearms resting on the back of the sofa. "I should certainly tell you that I have no interest in being spanked, thank you. That sort of behavior I leave to others."

Louisa couldn't resist running a hand over one warm firm buttock. "Too bad. I think we both might have enjoyed such an interlude. But that's not what I have in mind. For tonight, anyway…"

Her words hung on the air, enticing him, as she knew they would.

She kept her movements slow and deliberate, much as she would had she been training a skittish horse.

"Can you tell me what this is? Take a sniff…"

She held her hand under Owen's nose as he drew in a breath.

"It's spicy, um…seasoning. Oh yes—ginger. My housekeeper puts it into her suet pudding."

Louisa smiled.

"Correct, Owen. What do you know about ginger?"

As she asked this question, she reached for her small paring knife on a side table and began to peel and shape the root that was in her hand.

"Well, let me see. I know it came from the East. I remember reading somewhere about Queen Elizabeth liking it. It used to be very expensive."

"Do you like ginger, Owen?"

"I suppose so. I never thought very much about it."

"Good. I am going to use this ginger to help you feel things."

"You are?"

Louisa smiled at his tone of voice. It was as if Owen was three parts nervous and two parts intrigued.

"I grew this particular root myself, in case you are interested." Her fingers continued to work the root into the shape she desired. Scarcely longer than her thumb, with a flange at one end.

"Ah," said Owen, shifting slightly.

"There we are," finished Louisa. "Now we begin."

She moved behind Owen and spread his buttocks apart gently.

"What in the blue blazes—"

"Hush, Owen. I will not hurt you," said Louisa.

"But…I never…you shouldn't…" His protestations tapered off as Louisa gently slid her hands between his legs and caressed his balls. In spite of himself he moaned.

Louisa gently continued her stimulation, now pressing the ginger root against his tightly puckered flesh. He clenched in response to her touch.

"Owen, relax. This will be a pleasant experience for you—I would never hurt you."

She felt his efforts as his muscles slowly unclamped.

The carefully peeled ginger root slid past his ring of tight muscles and into his anus.

His breath came out with a whoosh.

"There, does that hurt?"

He carefully shook his head.

"It feels strange," he muttered.

"Now stand up, Owen." Louisa helped him stand and turned him toward her.

"What do I do now?"

"Nothing. I do it all from now on. You just let me know if you *feel* anything."

* * * * *

Well now, here was an interesting conundrum. He had something resembling a root vegetable shoved up his arse and she wanted to know if he *felt* anything.

He wanted to snort his incredulity, but had to admit that a slight sensation of warmth was beginning to infiltrate his entire pelvic area. His cock was already erect, but now his balls and buttocks were tingling.

Then he felt the warm moist swipe of her tongue around his cock and the top of his head nearly blew off.

"Louisa," he gasped, trying to resist the urge to thrust forward into her willing mouth.

"Hush now. You cannot feel anything, remember?"

Her breath wafted over his wet cock like static electricity, with much the same result. His cock stood up even more.

He was helpless to stop his hands from reaching down to her head and positioning her in just the right spot. Not that she needed much help, because her movements were deepening. She raised her hands to his backside and was pressing his cheeks tightly together as she moved his cock in and out of her mouth.

The warmth from the ginger became a sizzle. It was both arousing and stimulating. It made him wonder if his balls might be radiating enough heat to be glowing, and he was losing himself in the sensation.

Her tongue flickered over his most delicate tissue, leaving a path of dampness that felt exquisite as she drew her lips across it. She pushed his buttocks tighter, holding them closed with one hand now, as she used the other to hold his cock steady.

He could smell the ginger on her hands, mixed with the smell of her own sexual arousal, and the combined fragrances were making him dizzy.

His arse was burning now, not painfully but so close to it that his whole pelvis tightened with the heat. The scientist in him was busily cataloging the sensations, noting that the oils within the ginger root were probably coating his delicate inner tissues and sending the burning warmth deep into his body.

The man in him was simply trying his hardest to handle a unique sensation within his cock and balls. He wanted her tongue to swirl over his cock forever, he wanted to force himself as deeply as he could into her soft mouth, and pull himself out against that incredible vacuum her lips constantly created.

As if reading his mind, Louisa's mouth sucked at him, going deeper than he'd thought possible. She was pulling him practically down her throat, and he was sweating for control. His spine was beginning to tingle, his balls were a single taut lump, his knuckles were fisted in her hair and he rolled his head from side to side in an effort to keep from losing his mind.

"Louisa..." he grunted through clenched teeth. "I cannot hold back..."

Her only response was to draw him to the back of her throat and suck even more strongly, while caressing his ever-tightening balls.

His head swam, his heart pounded, and he wondered if he might actually be dying. Louisa's hand clamped his buttocks together, sending even more of the ginger's juices into his fragile flesh. Her mouth refused to leave his cock, and she held it tightly, pushing down into the hair surrounding it as her head moved rhythmically from base to tip.

His legs began to tremble as Louisa's mouth kept up its suckling movements on his swollen cock. His hands left her head and grasped the sofa back on either side of his hips as he spread his legs wide apart and gave himself up to the rushing of heat and desire within him. His arse ached with sexual tension, and his fists clenched as his entire world focused down to one woman's tongue on his cock.

He wanted to scream.

He wanted to come.

He did both.

Chapter 4

For the first time in her life, Louisa Cellini was scared.

It had been two weeks since that eventful night, when she had given Owen the best orgasm she could.

He didn't know that she'd come too.

It was an experience that rocked her world to its foundations, and threatened her very soul. Never had she come without some kind of stimulation. Never had she even considered the possibility that bringing pleasure to another might result in gaining such pleasure oneself.

Even now, a fortnight later, she had but to close her eyes to remember the taste and feel of him, in her mouth, under her hands, near her body. Her juices would flow at the thought of his scent and her clit would tighten and ache.

His shout at the moment of orgasm ranked as one of her greatest triumphs. She could still hear it ringing through her ears.

He'd come and come into her mouth, as if he'd saved himself for her alone. She'd relished every salty-creamy drop, because his movements beneath her hands had only heightened her own arousal.

Kneeling as she was, it was a simple matter for her to widen her stance and let the tension in her thighs pull the skin taut over her clit. Her rhythmic sucking had been echoed by a rhythmic clench within her cunt like nothing she'd ever experienced before. She found herself tightening her inner muscles as she tightened her tongue and lips, and when her nipples grazed Owen's hairy leg she almost gasped with the flash of sensation that snaked through her.

Within seconds of him coming, she'd dropped her hand, found her clit and with a mere touch, she was coming too. Erupting silently into shattering spasms that translated into gasps around Owen's cock and prolonged his orgasm as well.

Exhausted, Owen had collapsed onto the back of the sofa, panting for air. It had taken Louisa several moments to collect herself enough to get up off the floor and help him back to bed.

He was clearly still weak from the effects of his injuries, because within seconds of putting his head on the pillow, he'd slept.

Louisa had gently removed the ginger, eliciting only a murmur from him as she rolled him onto his stomach and covered him with the blankets.

From that moment on, she'd not gone near him.

She faced the truth—she was afraid.

Afraid that he'd come to mean something to her, something she didn't need or want. Afraid that she was no longer young and beautiful, and that if he ever did regain his sight, he'd take one look at her and head for London within the hour. Afraid that that was a pain she'd never be able to withstand.

Afraid that he wouldn't want her the way she wanted him. That he wouldn't crave her touch, her scent, her body, the way she craved his. That he wouldn't spend every waking moment wondering if they might ever come together again in the heat of lust and desire.

Louisa was definitely afraid. Afraid she might be falling in love.

* * * * *

Owen Lloyd-Jones was angry. Angry and afraid.

It had been two weeks since the most incredible night of his life and he hadn't seen hide nor hair of Louisa since.

And the main word there was "seen," because the morning following their encounter, Owen had opened his eyes and caught his first exciting glimpse of blurry movement.

Thrilled, he'd lain in bed waiting for Louisa, eager to share his news.

But she'd stayed away.

Her servants said she was busy, on estate business or county affairs or neighborly visits, but that she regularly inquired as to his progress.

Stubbornly, he refused to share this world-shattering improvement with anyone but her. If she couldn't be bothered to come and see for herself, why should he bother to tell anyone?

Each day, a little more light pierced the damaged surface of Owen's eyes, and he started finding it harder not to reveal his returning sight. None would know before Louisa, even if he had to go and drag her out from wherever she was hiding and tell her so.

Beneath his bravado, however, was fear.

Had he disgusted her with his sexual performance?

Not many women of his albeit limited acquaintance would consider taking a man into their mouths at all, let alone bringing him to the most shattering orgasm of his entire life and then continuing to suck him until he was spent and sated.

Even fewer women would have known to heighten such an orgasm with the clever use of spices. He still got hard just thinking about *that* part of it.

And she'd received nothing in return, just the limp and exhausted body of a well-used man who had promptly dropped off and enjoyed twelve of the best hours of sleep in his entire life. He didn't remember losing the ginger or his blindfold, but in the morning they'd been gone.

So where was she?

How was he going to be able to say all the things he wanted to say if she never came near him again?

How was he going to do all the things he wanted to do if she refused to visit him?

He had been allowed a few short walks from his room into a sitting room, and from there a brief stroll on the arm of a servant outside on the attached stone balcony.

The sun had felt exquisite, and the fact that he could now make out colors, shapes and movements heightened his enjoyment.

There was only one fly in the ointment—Louisa.

Owen spent quite a lot of time over the next days sitting quietly in front of the open veranda doors, listening to the song of the birds and enjoying the fragrances that blew in.

Funny how he had come to find all his senses improved by this recent experience. He could now distinguish between the delicate apple blossom scent and that of the azaleas that were just coming into bloom. He detected the newly scythed lawns as the first growth was cut, and occasionally an earthy whiff of horses and the stables made its way to his eager nose. He heard individual birds, although recognized few, and the warmth of the sun on his skin was a balm to his troubled thoughts. But above all, he could sense Louisa. Her fragrance was all around him, in his bedding, in the rooms he walked slowly through, and in the very air he breathed.

Something deep inside his heart recognized the scent, something that told him this was not merely a woman, but *his* woman. His common sense argued chemistry, his cock countered with passion.

He knew that Louisa was special. Special to him as a healer, as a selfless giver of herself.

He wanted to find out how much more special she was. He wanted to find out if she felt anything for him at all.

Above all, he wanted to find out how she'd feel tightened around his cock and heaving beneath him as he made her come over and over again.

Professor Owen Lloyd-Jones, noted scientist and brilliant deductive mind, began to plot.

Chapter 5

"Will there be anything else this evening, Sir?" politely inquired Jeffries, Louisa's efficient butler. He was just about finished clearing away the remnants of Owen's nightly bath.

"No, thank you, Jeffries. Have a pleasant night."

"You too, Sir."

Owen tamped down his excitement. Today the trap had been set, it was now awaiting the prey before it sprung and captured her—hopefully in his bed, beneath him.

He'd managed to carefully assemble the items he required. Apparently casual requests for oil of peppermint and a bottle of cloves came under the heading of "indigestion thanks to lack of exercise," and his evening request for hot water became routine. No one thought anything about it any more.

It was amazing to him exactly how much leeway an apparently blind person was allowed. He'd been left to himself for many an hour, at which time he'd had chance to rummage through his hostess's belongings like a thief in the night.

But he'd not stolen, merely borrowed. A long cord now rested beneath his pillow, as did a silk scarf.

Absently he popped a small clove into his mouth and chewed, freshening his breath and heating his tongue at the same time.

His silk robe chafed his anxious skin as he paced the room, praying that his scheme might work and bring her to him. His cock was twitching, already half aroused, and getting harder by the minute.

He slipped a couple of cloves into the hot water and inhaled as their pungent scent wreathed around the room. Owen realized he really enjoyed this part—the blending of the herbs and the creation of fragrance.

His message had been relayed, said Jeffries. Miss Louisa had been informed that Professor Lloyd-Jones was hesitant about trespassing on her hospitality further, and would be pleased to take his leave shortly. Could she visit for a short time this evening to discuss the matter?

Miss Louisa had agreed. She would do herself the honor of visiting Professor Lloyd-Jones after dinner, at the hour of half-past nine. Would that be acceptable to the Professor?

The Professor wanted to leap with joy but didn't, restricting himself to a businesslike nod of the head.

A clock sounded half-past nine. Where was she?

There—he heard it. His temporary blindness had increased his hearing skills to the point where he knew a foot had just been placed on the squeaky top step of the grand staircase. Not Jeffries, either, but a lighter foot. Her foot.

Gathering his supplies and his nerve, he got himself into position and waited.

* * * * *

Louisa was fighting the urge to run flying back down the stairs, out into the night and scream her pain.

Owen was leaving.

It was inevitable, but she had no idea it would hurt as much as it did. Years of self-control came to her aid, however, as she walked firmly up the last step and down the hallway leading to his door.

No one would ever guess the amount of strength it required for her to raise her hand and knock.

"Enter." His voice was firm and sent shivers through Louisa.

She opened the door quietly, surprised as she stepped through and did not immediately see Owen.

She was even more surprised when a pair of strong arms grasped her from behind and proceeded to lash her hands together with a silk cord. One of *her* silk cords, too.

"What the...Owen, what are you doing?" she squawked, taken aback by shock and aroused beyond measure by the feel of his arms around her. He rubbed his biceps deliberately across her breasts.

"Making *you* feel," he answered with a grin. "It's time I said thank you for what you've done for me. And what better way than by returning the favor you did me?"

She was now lashed, wrist to wrist, and she raised her eyes to his.

"Dear god, you can see!"

"Clever lady. If you had cared to come and visit me before, I'd have been able to share my progress with you. I've improved daily, my dear Louisa. You were right. It was temporary. Perhaps still blurry now and again, but to echo your words, yes. I can see."

Instead of struggling against her bonds, Louisa closed her eyes against the glow she saw deep in Owen's.

"Don't look at me like that," she whispered.

"Why not, Louisa?" he breathed, stroking her cheeks and her neck and down to her cleavage which rose above her low-cut gown.

"You're looking at me as if you desire me. I don't want anyone to want me. I've made a life without that kind of involvement. I don't want the pain that comes with wanting, needing, someone like that."

"And is it a satisfactory life, Louisa? Can it give you what I can give you?

His lips followed his fingers over her skin and she lifted her chin to give him access.

"It's the only life I know. It is tranquil, calm, it is what I always imagined life should be."

"Ah, but there's so much more for a woman like you, one who is passionate, sensual, just crying out for a man to touch her, a woman who will take a man's hand and pleasure herself against it."

Louisa jumped. "You were awake, you—you devil."

"Not really. I thought I had dreamed the feel of you until I woke and found that scent on my hand. Your scent, Louisa. It haunts me. I want it on my hands again. I want it on my lips and in my mouth and in the air I breathe."

Owen continued his gentle touching, reaching his hands behind her and loosening her laces. "Most of all I want it on my cock."

She humphed out a cynical sound. "I am a realist, Owen. My age shows in my body. When you could not see, I could pretend I was young and lovely, that my touch inflamed you. But now you can see what I am. No longer the young beauty who might bewitch you."

Owen's eyes narrowed at the pain in her voice.

"Suppose you allow me the privilege of making my own decisions on that score. Am I not adult enough to say what pleases me and what does not?"

Louisa raised her chin and opened her eyes, allowing her desire to overcome her fear of loving him too much.

"Very well. But don't say I didn't warn you. I understand you wish to leave. So perhaps this is the best way to say goodbye. With us seeing each other as we really are, not as our minds wish we might be."

Owen smiled. "Good idea."

He slipped her dress down from her shoulders and with one wrench tore it away from her bound wrists.

"Come, Louisa, follow me."

He pulled her to the bed and laid her gently down, looping the cord that tied her hands through the wooden carvings of the headboard. Then he removed the scarf from under the pillow.

"What...how did you..."

He stopped her mouth with a kiss. Their first.

His lips were warm and firm, and Louisa thought for a moment she'd die of the pleasure. He tasted of spices and his tongue eagerly sought hers as she parted her lips for his entrance.

She felt warmth against her naked breasts and realized his robe had fallen open and he was pressing himself against her body. God, she could come just from having him do this to her.

But he was just beginning.

The silk scarf went round her head and over her eyes.

"Now I have the edge, Louisa," he chuckled, his breath caressing her as he bent to flick his tongue quickly over a nipple.

Her body arched off the bed. He took immediate advantage of that fact by pulling the remnants of her gown away from her, leaving her nude before his hungry eyes.

Owen's hands ran down her body, learning her softness, testing her responses and making her growl under his touch.

"Beautiful, Louisa, beautiful," he muttered, sliding his palms over her thighs and up her hipbones to cup her breasts.

"How can you say that?" she whispered. "I know what I am..."

"Do you?" His fingers teased her nipples, and he chuckled as she moaned for him.

"Did you know that you have the most beautiful breasts?"

"Hah."

"Really. They are what a woman's breasts should be. Round, and full, and heavy enough to fit my hand while I hold them and do this..."

She felt his breath as his mouth neared her aroused flesh. Nerves aquiver, she waited for that first touch—when it came she wanted to sob.

He flicked, then licked, and then sucked, bringing more moans from Louisa's throat. The touch of his tongue was bliss. Her body wanted to leap off the bed, but Owen's warm weight was pressing into her.

His hands rose to either side of her breasts and he pressed inwards, bringing her nipples close enough for him to tease both with his mouth. He hummed with pleasure.

Louisa's heart pounded with the thrill and she ached to touch him, but her restraints held her in position, pushing her breasts upwards and into his waiting caresses.

She could feel the hot length of his cock against her leg, and knew her cunt was running freely, the honeyed juices begging for his touch.

She writhed, her blindfold heightening her awareness of every square inch of her skin.

And Owen knew. She knew he knew!

He raised himself away from her for a moment and she heard the clink of a glass.

Then he bent to kiss her and her mouth was suddenly filled with the icy hot taste of peppermint oil.

She sucked in a breath as he moved back and hissed as the air hit the peppermint in her mouth.

"Suck me, Louisa, oil my cock with your peppermint tongue."

She felt the bed dip and then the touch of his cock on her lips. Instinctively she opened her mouth wide, welcoming him in like a cherished treat.

Enthusiastically, she bathed his cock with the oil he'd pushed into her mouth. He felt so exquisite between her lips, so warm and velvety. She knew what he looked like and her mind conjured sensual images of her lying bound and blindfolded beneath him. His buttocks would be clenching as he grasped his cock and slid it into her waiting mouth. She suckled, covering as much of him as she could with her tongue and the peppermint oil.

"Easy, Louisa, here's a little more..."

She realized that more oil was dripping down his cock and into her mouth. She swirled it around him, knowing that from this moment on peppermint would be forever associated in her mind with this delicious experience.

She was slightly disappointed as he pulled away with a groan.

"Enough—we have a ways to go yet."

The bed moved again and she jumped as she felt him part her thighs. Her clit ached and she could feel the moisture that had pooled all around her hot and swollen entrance.

The touch of his tongue surprised a loud gasp from deep in her throat.

He'd coated his tongue with peppermint oil as well, and the feel of the cooling heat over her slick cunt was rapture defined.

"Mmmm..." he murmured, sending vibrations up and down her spine. "Tasty woman."

His tongue learned her every crease and fold, lapping her juices and spreading the peppermint oil all around. He must have known how sensitive she was because he did not touch her clit with his coated tongue, but the strokes to either side were enough to make her see stars.

When he moved away she nearly cried out with loss.

"Don't worry, my sweet, there's more where that came from."

She felt a cool trickle of liquid over her mound, and then the strangely hot and cold blast of the peppermint oil he'd poured. He bent again to his task, this time filling her cunt with his tongue and thrusting the peppermint oil as far as he could into her heat.

"Turnabout is fair play, Louisa," he said, sliding one oily finger through her cleft to her puckered ring of sensitive muscles. Her buttocks clenched.

She could hear the smile in his voice and somewhere deep inside of her a little knot of ice began to melt. He wouldn't be doing this if he didn't have some feelings for her. She relaxed and let him caress her most delicate entrance, the peppermint oil heightening the amazing sensation.

Once again he moved.

She felt his hands pressing on the bed close to her arms and sensed his full weight surrounding her. The heat from his body was intense and she thrust her hips upwards in mute invitation.

The invitation was accepted. Thoroughly.

The long, thick, pepperminty cock of Professor Owen Lloyd-Jones slid past the entrance and buried itself perfectly within the hot and silky cunt of Miss Louisa Cellini.

Chapter 6

Louisa stilled.

He was deep inside her, and their mingled juices and oils were both stimulating and deadening the effect.

"Owen…" she whispered.

"I know, my love, I know."

His love? He'd called her his *love*? Did he mean it? Why did he have to pick this very moment to say that? Just when she wanted to savor these sensations he had to go and toss that out, distracting her mightily. Was it possible that he too was stirred by this mating, this joining, this *incredible* fuck?

She wanted to ask him, and was searching for the words when he moved. Any further conscious thought evaporated from her mind.

He pulled back almost to the tip of his cock and then stroked back in, even deeper than before. His groan of pleasure was echoed in her heart, and she moaned with him as he repeated the stroke.

Owen reached for her bonds and within seconds she was free to grasp his shoulders, his back, and his buttocks. Her hands were everywhere.

He maintained his steady thrusting, always pushing a little further, touching her clit with his groin and brushing her with his tight curls.

Spirals of tension coiled themselves around her cunt. The peppermint oil had increased the sensation of the air that was being forced away from their straining bodies. Louisa was spellbound by the effect.

Her mound alternately blazed and chilled, in time with Owen's thrusts.

He bent his head and suckled fiercely on her breast, adding more stimuli to her sensual torment.

She was almost there.

Once again, Owen seemed to know.

He withdrew and left her sobbing with the need to come.

"Soon, my sweet, soon…" he whispered.

His hands untied her blindfold and with a smooth motion he flipped her onto her stomach.

Unhesitatingly she raised her bottom, presenting herself to him, begging for the release he'd denied her.

"Yes, Louisa, oh yes…" His hands gripped her hips, and he plunged his length back inside her eager cunt.

She cried out her relief at having his hard length back where it belonged. His fingers tightened on her buttocks and her cheeks spread. He touched the tissues around her anus with his fingers, spreading more oil and driving her into a state of temporary insanity.

She mewled, she cried, she writhed, her body was no longer her own, but Owen's to do with as he would. And he played it like a virtuoso on a favorite instrument.

The peppermint oil had numbed their tissues slightly, and it seemed that Owen could now last forever. His strokes were powerful, but controlled, and he deliberately tilted her so that he could reach all her most sensitive places.

She pressed back against him fiercely, offering not only her body but her soul to this man who was taking her farther into ecstasy than she had ever imagined possible.

His hands caressed her sweating flesh, running over her hips, her buttocks, down her thighs and back up to slide across her mound.

She had been trembling on the edge of coming for so long that her muscles were now starting to throb, adding their own rhythmic accompaniment to the symphony Owen was playing on her senses.

Once again he withdrew, leaving Louisa hoarse and tighter than a newly strung bow.

He slid around and beneath her, positioning her right above his swollen and gleaming cock.

"Now, Louisa. I can see you. Let me see you as you come. Share that secret with me," he urged.

His hands went to her hips and she unhesitatingly lowered herself down, down onto his wonderful cock.

For a moment she sat there, feeling him deeper inside than he'd ever gone before. She raised her eyes to his, asking questions for which there might be no answers.

His gaze told her everything she needed to know. This moment meant as much to him as it did to her. His lids were lowered and his eyes on fire with desire as he watched her. His lips were parted and swollen from their kisses, his nipples as hard as hers, and his whole body rigid with his need for her.

Owen wanted her, no doubts, no hesitations. He wanted *her*.

Well, he could have her.

She began to move, slowly at first, riding him in languorous strokes of her silky cunt up and down his heat.

But it was not enough for either of them.

Owen raised his hands to tease her nipples and she gasped at the pleasure.

Louisa reached for his balls and stroked them gently. He moaned at the blissful shivers she induced.

Both of them knew the end was close.

Louisa's movements became jerkier as Owen's hand found her clit and gently stimulated the sensitive nubbin while she rode him.

Her hips rotated slightly and it was Owen's turn to moan. The rhythm they had initiated increased in speed and intensity.

Owen pushed himself up on his hands, using all his strength to bring himself level with Louisa.

She was in his lap, bound firmly to his chest by arms of steel and they were pounding against each other in their mutual need for fulfillment.

"Look at me, Louisa," grunted Owen. "I need to see your eyes as you come…"

His cock was somewhere in her deepest recesses, and her clit was grinding itself into his pubic bone. Her ankles were crossed behind his back and she held him to her with rigid muscles.

Her fingernails scored his shoulders and her eyes were fixed on his as her passions spiraled out of control.

"It's now, Owen…it's now…" she yelled.

"Yes, Louisa…let it go NOW."

Two voices cried out in orgasm. Two bodies spasmed against each other in release. Two hearts pounded in unison.

Two souls found bliss.

Chapter 7

The world slowly righted itself as the lovers untangled their trembling limbs and collapsed onto the bed.

Owen drew Louisa close to his heart, enfolding her in his arms and hugging her tight, refusing to allow her to withdraw from him even an inch.

"You are my mate. You know that, don't you?" he said, so matter-of-factly that he took Louisa's breath away.

She drew in a breath to respond, but a quick kiss sealed her lips.

"There has never been another woman in my life who has ever made me feel like that. Nor will there be. There has never been another woman who I have wanted to do things like that to. Nor will there be. Am I getting my point across at all?"

"You're not leaving?" asked Louisa hopefully.

Owen chuckled. "Not unless you want me to. And probably not even then. You're mine, Louisa. Heart, body—and lovely body it is—" he squeezed her for emphasis, "-and soul. Marry me?"

Louisa was, for probably the first and only time in her life, at a loss for words.

"I'll take that as a yes," grinned Owen, kissing her again.

"But...but..." she stuttered.

"What buts? We've found each other, Louisa. I've spent four decades of my life alone. I'm going to spend the next four with you, if you'll have me..."

"If I'll *have* you?" Louisa's voice returned with enthusiasm. "Have you? I'll *have* you every day, every hour, right this minute, if you want. I've never felt this way about any man, never wanted any man in my life but you, Owen. "

Her hips ground against him in emphasis.

"If you're serious, I'll happily spend the next four decades with you and all the ones after those as well." She laughed with joy as he pulled her against him and kissed her once more.

"And Owen?"

He looked lovingly at her.

"I have a special room I can't wait to show you."

Epilogue

"Auntie Weeza, Auntie Weeza, lookeeeee…"

A young voice echoed around the delightful parterre of Montvale House as young Master Jonathan Barbour galloped past the ornamental pond. Proud as punch of his new hobbyhorse, Jonathan was spending long hours in the saddle. This pleased his parents enormously for two reasons. Firstly, Lord Nicholas Barbour had created the wooden toy all on his own, and secondly, young Jonathan was so tired that he dropped right off to sleep when tucked in to bed at night. This allowed Nick and his wife, Miranda, more hours of uninterrupted pleasure.

"Auntie Weeza" looked on with a smile.

"That child is an endless fount of energy," laughed Beatrice, Countess of Dunsmere, who was sitting next to Lady Miranda Barbour and Mrs. Louisa Lloyd-Jones.

"You don't need to tell me," said Miranda ruefully. "If the next one's as bad, I'm shutting Nick out of our bedroom for five years." She stroked her stomach protectively.

Louisa snorted. "I can't see that happening."

Miranda chuckled and returned Louisa's grin. "Well, no. You're right there. I like loving Nick far too much to ever shut him out. Strange, isn't it?"

"What is?" asked Beatrice, shifting her sleeping daughter from one arm to the other and leaning back against the cushions.

"How all three of us have ended up with the one thing we thought we'd never need or want, or indeed have—a man."

The ladies' eyes wandered to the side of the garden where three gentlemen were deeply involved in something on a stone table.

Louisa grinned at the sight. "Owen has them working on his latest project, I see." She shaded her eyes. "One hopes that no one's fingers turn green at least..."

Beatrice and Miranda laughed with her, remembering Owen's last attempt at creating a fragranced soap which had resulted in a delicate shade of spring green dying everything that came in contact with it, including the pot boy.

"God, I love him so." Louisa's breath caught as a wave of emotion swamped her.

Beatrice's gaze fell to the softly snoring child in her arms. "I know dearest, I know. Harry and I are blessed with each other, and now to have little Mary Louise, well, it really is wonderful, isn't it?"

Miranda nodded, tears in her eyes, as the three women shared the depth of their feelings with a handclasp, a glance and a smile.

"So tell me, Louisa," said Miranda. "Have you decided what to do with your special room yet?"

Louisa laughed out loud, attracting the attention of her husband, whose head turned swiftly towards her. "Not yet. We're still having too much fun in there."

She watched as the three men strode towards their wives, strong, handsome and radiating contentment. Each couldn't wait to touch the woman that he had made his own. Nick's hand caressed Miranda's cheek, Harry bent to drop a light kiss on the top of Beatrice's head and stroke his daughter, and Owen—ah, Owen.

Arriving at Louisa's side, he grasped her by the waist, lifted her bodily out of the chair and planted a passionate kiss on her lips. His actions were appreciated by his wife who slid her arms about his neck and returned the kiss with enthusiasm.

A round of applause broke them apart, but neither looked ashamed. They just looked — happy.

THE END

PLEASURING MISS POPPY

Chapter 1

The soft scream that rolled across the grass informed Professor Owen Lloyd-Jones that his wife had achieved her pleasure beneath him. Both ignored the birds that fled from the trees above them and the squirrel that was watching them with nervous interest from a nearby branch.

With a final thrust, Owen buried himself to his balls inside Louisa and groaned as once again he lost himself inside this incredible woman.

They may have been married for nearly five years, but the thrill of claiming her would never fade.

She sighed as he withdrew and lay beside her, one arm possessively beneath her breasts and his nose buried against her neck.

He'd never imagined he could love anyone as much as he loved Louisa.

"Tired, sweetheart?"

She turned and smiled at him, her sleepy contentment warming his heart. "A little. But not from this." A wicked grin curved her lips. "I'm never too tired for *this*..." She ran her hand up her husband's lean flank. "It's just that it was a trying morning. This fete is turning out to be an exercise in diplomacy as much as an exercise in organization."

"Mrs. Polgarry again?"

"Not this time." Louisa laughed. "I had to convince Mrs. Dunford that she couldn't judge the pickle contest by herself. Then she objected to Jane Clapham, and so I threw in another woman to even the mix and they are now a committee for the pickle judging. God help us."

Owen smiled. "You're doing too much, love."

Louisa shook her head. "I adore doing this every year, Owen, and you know it. By tomorrow the village green will be full of merrymakers, everyone will have a wonderful time, and by the next day—it'll all be over."

Owen idly ringed his wife's nipple with one finger. "The village certainly loves it." He dropped a kiss on the soft and puckered skin. "I suppose we'll be afflicted with Squire Adams and his family again?"

"I'm afraid so. He and Dorothea wouldn't miss the chance to lord it over the locals. I hear their eldest daughter is back home too. She didn't *take* in London, and Dorothea is desperate to marry her off." Louisa's mouth pursed. "Poor thing."

Owen sat up and began to tug his clothes back on. It was time for them both to head back to their duties. Although he'd rather head to his laboratory, he knew Louisa loved having him share in the preparation for their midsummer fete at Montvale House. So he tidied up his experiments, put his notes away and spent two weeks helping.

The price was, of course, plenty of stolen moments for some passionate lovemaking. Like they'd just enjoyed.

He tied his wife's laces thoughtfully. "Perhaps the Squire's daughter will meet someone tomorrow."

Louisa shook her head. "To listen to Dorothea talk, this girl is destined to be a Countess. They're determined to snag a title for her."

Owen sighed. "So silly. Let the girl find her happiness, not some meaningless title."

"Like we did?" Louisa glanced impishly over her shoulder as Owen knotted the last lace.

"Look at me like that again, love, and we'll find some more. But we'll be dreadfully late, you'll have more twigs in your hair…" He removed two. "And everyone will know what we've been up to."

Louisa chuckled. "I don't care particularly, but I did promise to oversee the setup of the pie table. I suppose we must return."

Owen helped her stand, brushed off her gown and let his hands linger on her buttocks. "Finish early," he growled. "I have a few *experiments* I'd like to research further. Time for a little play in our room, I'm thinking."

Louisa shivered under his gaze. Doubtless she knew exactly what he was talking about. Her secret room, with its vast collection of sexual toys, had become a favorite spot for both of them.

"Without a doubt, my curious love. I'm always willing to participate in a little…*research*." She pressed herself against him for a long moment and let her lips brush his.

Then, slowly drawing back, she linked her arm through Owen's, and they strolled back towards Montvale House and their assigned tasks for the afternoon.

Neither noticed a figure lurking in the hedgerow, watching them exchange loving touches and smiles.

* * * * *

The annual Montvale Summer Fete was in full swing. Tables groaned under the weights of pies, homemade pickles, and other assorted foods, the quoits field had attracted a lot of visitors, and a noisy game of Blind Man's Bluff was underway for the children.

Chatter and laughter filled the air as Louisa and Owen strolled arm-in-arm through the merrymakers.

A pig was turning slowly over an open fire, and the scents of roast pork mingled with the soft summer breezes.

Louisa was pleased to see that all seemed to be progressing smoothly. She had reservations about the evening to come, since the barrel of rough cider would be added to the local brewmaster's table, and probably drained thoroughly. But by that time, she and Owen would be back in Montvale House, and those who chose to drink themselves into a stupor could do so with no help from either of them.

"Ah, Professor Lloyd-Jones, Mrs. Lloyd-Jones...lovely day, what what?"

Louisa winced at the booming voice, and she felt the little shudder as Owen clenched his teeth. Squire Adams was bearing down on them.

"Dorothea, come and make your greetings. Here's our lovely hostess." The Squire showed large amounts of teeth.

"Oh Mrs. Lloyd-*Jones*. *Professor*. Such a wonderful day for the Fete. I was telling my good friend the other day, the dear *Duchess* Granditon you know, about the splendid job you always do..."

The large woman in the improbably purple gown gushed over Louisa. Her compliments were flowery and profuse and Louisa would bet her best dildo that she didn't mean a word of them. Three girls trailed in her wake like foam behind a boat.

"You will recall my girls, of course." She waved a hand at her entourage. "But you haven't met our eldest daughter." Mrs. Adams glanced around with a frown. "Drat the girl. Poppy? Where's Poppy?" She turned and glared at her remaining daughters. "Have any of you seen Poppy?"

"No Mama," they chorused.

Louisa gazed at the assembled froth. Somewhere along the line, the Squire's wife had equated ruffles with gentility. She could barely make out the girls, so smothered were they in lace and tulle.

"Oh *there* she is." Mrs. Adams clicked her tongue. "Drawing again, I'll warrant. How am I to get that girl a husband when all she does is bury her head in her sketchpad? I ask you." She narrowed her lips. "Children can be such a trial,

Mrs. Jones." Her eyes narrowed too. "Oh, I forget. Of course, you don't *have* any do you?"

Owen, always quick to respond to anything he perceived as a slight to his wife, stepped into the conversation. "Well, Mrs. Adams, we certainly manage to enjoy our friends' children. Lord and Lady Barbour's son Jonathon is our godchild, you know. And of course there's the Count and Countess of Dunsmere…we understand they're about to add twins to their family." He turned to Louisa with a smile. "More little ones to keep us busy, my love."

Mrs. Adams huffed, quite out-trumped by this parade of titles, as Owen had obviously known she would be.

"Well, that's as it may be. You simply *must* meet Poppy, though."

Louisa glanced over to the quiet and shady corner where a mass of pink ruffles sat on the grass, holding a small piece of paper.

"*Poppy*?" The screech rattled Louisa's teeth, and her heart went out to the poor girl who had evidently escaped her family's presence for a few moments of relaxation. The pink ruffles fluttered, and a dark head jerked upwards.

With an awkward move, the girl stood, and Louisa noticed a twist of paper fall to the ground behind her.

Slowly she approached, shoulders slumped, and as she neared, Louisa tilted her head and took a good look at her. The real girl, not the beruffled and beribboned creature her mother was presenting to the world.

Poppy Adams was not what she appeared. Louisa was convinced of it, and her hand tightened a little on Owen's sleeve.

Even slumped, the girl was above average height. Her mahogany hair had been teased into an awful mess of ringlets around her face, almost hiding the creamy complexion.

Her gown, in Louisa's stylish opinion, should have been taken out somewhere and shot. Besides the ruffles that made her seem like a circus figure, it was too tight, forcing her breasts up into an unnatural position. And they were not small breasts. Ribbons flew everywhere, and Louisa had never seen a more miserable face in her life.

She ached. Here was a woman that was being squashed, literally *and* figuratively, into a mold that didn't fit her. Something inside Louisa stirred to life. She had no maternal instincts, as far as she knew, but this poor child needed *something*.

Mrs. Adams sighed. "Poppy? Come here. You must make yourself known to our host and hostess." Her voice dropped. "And do it *properly*, girl."

Louisa caught the admonition and her resolution firmed.

"Good day, Professor Jones, Mrs. Jones."

Poppy's voice was low and soft, and she gave a half-hearted curtsey, which earned her a stern glare from her mother.

"Isn't she adorable? It's the *London* touch, of course. She's been there for several months, but we couldn't *bear* to be without her on such a festive occasion."

Louisa didn't miss the expression that twisted Poppy's lips into a tiny pucker of distaste. "Did you enjoy your stay in London, my dear?"

"No…I mean yes," stuttered Poppy, as her mother gave her a none-too-subtle dig in the ribs. "It was, of course, all things perfect. Especially the art galleries…"

"Oh there you go *again*." Mrs. Adams interrupted Poppy with a shrill giggle. "Such a silly thing, isn't she? All the parties, the beaux, Almacks, dancing 'til dawn, and what does my little girl do? Waste time at some stuffy art museum." Mrs. Adam's laugh was anything but fond. "*Girls*. What *is* a mother to do?"

Louisa thought for a moment. "Poppy, we have some quite nice paintings up at Montvale House. Might we be able to convince your mother to let you visit with us and view them?"

The girl's face lit up. A fine pair of grey eyes sparkled. *Aaah. There she is,* thought Louisa. *The real Poppy Adams.*

Mrs. Adams was gushing again. "Oh my, Mrs. Jones. How kind, how benevolent. To take a poor country girl into your home...well, we're overwhelmed by your gentility." She glared at Poppy again. "*Aren't* we?"

Poppy curtseyed again. "Indeed, Ma'am. You are too gracious."

"Not at all," smiled Louisa. "My husband and I both enjoy fine works of art. It will be a pleasure for us to share them. Shall we say around four today?"

Poppy let a small smile of acknowledgement cross her features and nodded.

The groups separated, and Owen glanced down at his wife. "What was all that about?"

Louisa grinned. "I think we may have found ourselves a small treasure, Owen. The frame is dreadful, and the whole thing needs cleaning up a bit, but I have a very strong feeling that there's more to Miss Poppy Adams than meets the eye."

She stooped and quietly retrieved a small, crumpled piece of paper. "If nothing else, I felt bad for the poor girl, having to endure a mother like that."

Owen nodded. "No arguments there. I was seriously thinking of asking that woman to volunteer as the target for today's archery contest. But then I realized that would be unfair, since there's so *much* of her a blind man could probably hit her."

Louisa giggled, then gasped as she smoothed out the folds from the sketch Poppy had dropped surreptitiously in the grass.

It was a quick pencil sketch. Two lovers, lying entangled with each other, their bodies straining for release and their muscles taut against the grass beneath them.

"Well, well," she said thoughtfully. "It would seem I was right. There is a great deal more to Miss Poppy Adams than might appear on the surface."

She held out her hand and showed Owen the sketch.

"Look, darling. It's us."

Chapter 2

Damian Barbour scowled as he paced the hallway of Montvale House. He'd ridden very carefully around the country fair that seemed to be in full swing in a nearby field, since there was nothing he could imagine enjoying *less*.

He was still seriously pissed off at his cousin Nick for demanding he vacate London immediately.

So what if he'd been in bed with two women? Hell, Nick had probably done that a score of times himself before tying himself up to Miranda. She was a good sort, and Damian liked her, but hell.

And so what if they'd been the mistresses of two of the most powerful men in Parliament? If they couldn't satisfy their own women, and he, Damian, could, why should Nick get in such a twitter over the whole thing?

He snorted. It was downright stupid and narrow minded of Nick to exile him all the way to Yorkshire until the fuss died down.

Of course, he adored Louisa and Owen. They'd welcomed him on the occasions he'd accompanied Nick and Miranda up here, and they'd all had a good time together. The shooting was great in the winter, Louisa was as outspoken and delightful as a woman could be, and Owen's work was fascinating.

But still…

Damian's cock stirred at the thought of the bodies he'd left panting and sated in that elegant salon. He sighed. So perhaps the Calderton's ball hadn't been the best place to indulge, but when the opportunity arose, so did Damian.

He grinned. It certainly had been fun.

He prowled the all-but-silent house, wondering where he'd be sleeping. And possibly with whom, if there were any suitable candidates about.

Aha.

A woman was staring at a framed print on the wall. A maid by the look of that god-awful ruffled dress, probably handed down from her mistress. Her head was slightly tilted, and a nice pair of breasts was pushing against the tightly laced front of her bodice.

Damian licked his lips. He'd just bet they'd spill out into his hands in abundance when he released them.

It wasn't in his nature to fuck the servants, but surely a quick kiss wouldn't hurt. And he'd make sure she enjoyed it. He had no doubts about his abilities in *that* area.

"Fascinating, isn't it?" He kept his voice low as he came up behind her, and slid his arms around her, cupping those delicious breasts in his hands.

The woman froze, then quickly turned, and with a sharp movement raised her knee, catching him fair and square in the balls.

Damian crumpled to the floor.

"How *dare* you?" Her voice was filled with outrage.

Damian's lungs struggled for the breath she'd knocked out of him. He'd like to have explained, but seeing as his life was passing before his eyes and he thought he might vomit up his cock from where she'd lodged it in his throat, he was unable to respond.

He simply moaned.

"Damian? What the blazes..."

Louisa's voice echoed through the hall, and she rushed to the couple. "Good God, are you ill?"

Damian whimpered.

Louisa glanced at the girl. "Miss Adams...Poppy...are you all right?"

The girl's eyes widened. "Oh dear lord. Do you know him? I didn't realize...I thought when he touched...oh good grief." A rush of color spread over her creamy skin and she chewed her lip nervously.

Louisa's eyebrow rose. "Damian, you sod. You misbehaved, didn't you?"

Damian cleared his throat with difficulty. An urge to groan receded and he struggled to his feet, trying not to wince.

"Louisa, I..."

Louisa stared at him sternly and raised her hand. "No excuses. I can imagine what happened, and if Poppy hadn't done it, I probably would have. Will you *never* learn?"

Damian looked as shamefaced as a man clutching his genitals could be.

Louisa sighed. "Apologize to Miss Adams." She turned to Poppy. "This...*person*...is Lord Nick Barbour's cousin. Damian Barbour, Poppy Adams."

Poppy dropped a self-conscious curtsey.

Damian attempted a half-hearted bow. Not hard, since he was pretty much locked in that position anyway. At least for the next few minutes.

"Poppy is our *guest*, Damian, and even if she wasn't, what the hell were you thinking?"

That she has luscious tits. "I'm so sorry, Louisa. Miss Adams, I don't know what came over me. Seeing such beauty, just standing there alone..."

Poppy snorted inelegantly. "Oh quite. Seems Mr. Barbour has a tongue as quick as his hands."

Louisa tried to conceal her smile, and failed. "Well put, Poppy." She tipped her head to one side. "Reparations must be made, of course."

Damian blanched. "I say, Louisa...it was an honest mistake..."

She glared at him. "Honest or not, I must think about this situation. And *your* situation, Damian. Nick and Miranda wrote and told me the whole story."

A look of interest crossed Poppy's face, but Damian decided matters had gone far enough without going into the reasons for his trip to Yorkshire.

"I throw myself on your mercy, lovely Louisa. Punish me, beat me...I welcome the chance to make amends."

He put every ounce of charm he possessed into his very best smile and was pleased to see Louisa relax as he managed to straighten to his full height. Whether his cock would ever straighten again was another matter.

"You're a beast, Damian, but a delightful one. Come along, I'll show you to your room, and then Poppy and I can have a proper visit and look at the paintings."

Poppy drew aside as they passed, but Damian couldn't resist the opportunity to glance back at her.

Sharp grey eyes were fixed on him, and a slight shiver ran up his spine that had nothing to do with his aching balls.

He obeyed some inner impulse. He winked.

* * * * *

Poppy turned back to the painting and stared at it, not seeing a single thing. The masterfully-executed oil depicted the classic myth of the Judgment of Paris, but she was no longer entranced by the brushwork, or the artful way the painter had managed to convey beauty and strife in one canvas.

She was seeing blue eyes. Dimmed with the pain she'd inflicted on him, certainly, but bluer than she could have imagined eyes to be. And the rest of him was a good match.

Damian Barbour was one very good-looking man. If one liked tall men, with sandy colored hair, big shoulders, nicely formed thighs, a delicate touch and a pair of lips that looked just right for…

Poppy shook herself mentally. Time to stop daydreaming. There wasn't a chance in the world that he'd look at her again. She was a dowd, an art-obsessed, prune-faced chit, and had nothing at all to attract a man like Damian. Her mother had dinned that into her often enough.

"Don't expect to get swept off your feet by some handsome duke, girl. You must face realities. You're not a beauty, and never will be. Find yourself an older man with a title and marry him. It's your duty."

Her mother's words echoed in her ears and she winced, trying to use the beauty of the masterpiece before her to block them out.

Tears trembled, but before they could fall, Louisa returned. "Poppy, I'm so sorry…"

Louisa's voice reflected her concern, and Poppy felt surprised at the depth of her own response to such gentle reassurance. "I'm fine. Really. It was just a shock, that's all."

"Good girl." Louisa smiled and took her arm companionably. "Now tell me, what do you think of my paintings?"

The two women wandered for a while, and Poppy was surprised at the scope and intelligence of Louisa's opinions. Not only on art, but also on life itself. Feeling at ease with her hostess as they shared a tea tray, Poppy said so.

"Louisa, I envy you your knowledge."

"Of what, my dear?"

Poppy waved her hand. "Everything. Art, literature…*life*, I suppose."

"Why do you envy me? It will come to you in time."

"Not if my mother has her way." She stared at her empty teacup. "All I want to do is paint, Louisa. I am in heaven when that canvas is in front of me. But my mother..." She paused. "My mother objects to my subject matter."

Louisa moved and opened her small reticule, pulling out a crumpled piece of paper. "You mean like this?"

Poppy was aghast. "I...*Louisa*, I...didn't..."

Louisa laughed. "Darling, don't look so horrified. It's a wonderful drawing, and one I'll treasure. You've captured a special moment here, and the passion we felt is in every line you've drawn."

Poppy swallowed. "You're not *cross*?"

"Of course not. Why should I be?"

"But...but...Mama said I shouldn't...you...your husband...I mean I drew you *naked*."

"And very well too."

Poppy stared. "You think so?"

This was not what she'd been expecting at all. The first time she'd drawn a naked body, she'd received the beating of her life. Since then, she'd learned to keep her artwork in an assortment of hiding places, or, even worse, destroy them when she'd finished them.

"Indeed I do." Louisa leaned forward and placed her teacup gently on its saucer. "Poppy, you have a talent. That's beyond doubt. You need to accept it, and enjoy it."

"But...but..." Poppy's mind reeled. "I like to paint *nudes*," she sputtered.

"Yes, I know."

"And you're not horrified?"

Louisa's laugh rang out. "We're *all* nude underneath our clothing, my dear. I see nothing wrong with the human body in all its glory."

Poppy blinked. Her mouth worked once or twice but no sound came out.

Louisa chuckled again. "I have an idea, love. How would you like to spend a few days here at Montvale House with me? Now that the fete is over, Owen will be disappearing back to his laboratory to make up for lost time. I'd very much enjoy your company."

"I...I don't know what to say," breathed Poppy. If angels had appeared over Louisa's head and sounded their trumpets she probably wouldn't have been any more surprised. "It sounds like heaven."

"Good. I'll write a note to your Mama, and forgive me if I tell you that I will probably indulge in a small fib or two. You can stay here, spend some time with me, and perhaps even get in a little painting." Louisa's eyes widened naughtily. "And I think I might have just the model for you as well."

By now, Poppy's tongue had stuck to the roof of her mouth. To stay here, in an environment where she could speak her mind, freely, without fear of retribution. To exchange ideas with a woman who wasn't horrified at the idea of nudity. To *paint!*

Oh my.

The room swam a little, and Poppy blinked, trying to restore her vision. "I would...I would *love* that, Louisa."

The older woman grinned. "I have some interesting things to show you, in addition to the paintings we own—after dinner perhaps. We'll have some time to ourselves. I think you're the sort of woman who might appreciate my collection."

Poppy tilted her head inquiringly, but Louisa just smiled and rang for the servants.

Collection? What collection?

Life had suddenly become very intriguing, and Poppy's heart beat to a happy rhythm as she followed the servant out of the room to the chamber that would be hers for the next few days.

She intended to seize, devour and relish every single moment of this time.

God knew if she'd ever get the chance to do so again.

Chapter 3

Damian looked forward to dinner that evening. The little imp of mischief which had been his downfall throughout his life was anticipating teasing Miss Adams and making her blush.

But to his surprise, he was welcomed to the table by a self-possessed young woman, still looking rather a fright, but with all her wits about her.

Encouraged by Owen and Louisa, the conversation around the informal meal wandered through a variety of topics, from London reminiscences to the current state of political affairs and finally, inevitably, to the arts. The meal was accompanied by a fine wine, and as the glasses were refilled, everyone relaxed into the discussion.

As she expounded on the beauties of some of the artwork in the London Galleries, Damian covertly studied Poppy.

There was *something* there.

Something he couldn't quite put his finger on, but something that caught his attention and made him focus on her quite intently. Her hair was a mess, her dress appalling, and she was too tall.

She was a far cry from the petite blondes who were the toast of the Ton, and the word "elf" would never be used in the same sentence with Miss Poppy Adams.

But the light in her grey eyes, her obvious intelligence and her lack of self-consciousness as she unabashedly betrayed her knowledge of the art world, appealed to him on some fundamental level. Her casual acceptance of him as a dinner partner and her unalloyed appreciation of her third glass of wine were charming.

Here was a woman unafraid to demonstrate that she used her brains. She had no care that in some London salons her conversation would damn her as a "bluestocking" and send her to the fringes of the dance floor.

She used no wiles to attract *him*, the only eligible male at the table, in fact she rarely looked at him. But when she did, it was with a challenging glance, as if she really cared about what he was going to say.

Perhaps that was the difference. His interactions with women had, of late, revolved around one thing and one thing only. And he'd had plenty of it. Maybe a little too much. That first eye contact, followed by a touch to the sleeve, a hand slipped to the spine of a willing conquest, and the inevitable journey to the nearest darkened room or her quiet home, had become routine.

It would appear that simple fucking had begun to lose its appeal for Damian. Talking, listening, exchanging ideas and arguments, was something altogether new.

The conversation took on a level of sensuality all its own.

For the first time, Damian felt himself attracted to a woman on a different level. Poppy's vibrant enthusiasm for her topics, coupled with her rich laughter, were sending some interesting feelings through his body. He wanted to do some exploring of this woman. Physically—certainly, but the odd thought occurred to him that he might actually be able to hold a conversation with her afterwards.

He quirked an eyebrow at himself, wondering where the hell *that* notion had come from.

Since when had using his mouth for anything other than bringing screams to his bedmates become important? The pursuit, the conquest, the romp between the sheets, and then the polite departure followed by some small token of appreciation.

That was how the game worked. Or had done up to now.

Damian's mind drifted into strange and twisted pathways as he turned the problem over, and he was almost surprised when Louisa folded her napkin and rose.

"Gentlemen, Poppy and I will leave you to your port. Don't rush, since I have plans for us ladies that don't include you. Not until later, anyway."

She flashed a quick glance full of promise at Owen, and even Damian felt the heat. *Lucky Owen.*

"We'll say goodnight now, I think, and see you in the morning, Damian."

He and Owen rose and bowed the ladies out of the room.

Silence fell for a moment, as both men watched their departure.

"Interesting girl," mused Damian.

"Louisa thinks so." Owen stretched. "She's had an idea about our Miss Poppy. I'm supposed to explain it to you."

Damian glanced over at his friend.

Owen shrugged. "Just doing my husbandly duty. I think we'd better go and find that port. You might need it."

* * * * *

Poppy followed Louisa through Montvale House, letting her curiosity expand to a bubble of anticipation inside her. Louisa had mentioned a "collection". Perhaps this was now the time for her to see it? Jewelry perhaps? Miniatures?

The older woman paused before a bookshelf and slid a volume out, opening a cleverly-concealed door. She turned to Poppy.

"What you are about to see is the result of many years of acquisition, by old Lord Montvale, and by myself. Both when I was his mistress and ever since."

Poppy blinked. "You were…his mistress?"

Louisa smiled. "Long before I met and married Owen, but yes." She stepped through into the dimly lit room. "Are you shocked?"

Poppy examined her thoughts critically, surprising herself with her answer. "No."

"Good."

Louisa lit more candles and an astounding sight met Poppy's eyes. The room was filled with an assortment of objects, books and artwork, all geared towards the enjoyment of sexual pleasure. It was comfortable, curious and quite large, with an elegant fireplace at one end.

"Good lord," breathed Poppy. She didn't know where to look first.

Louisa stoked up the fire, and Poppy noticed an enormous hipbath steaming in one corner.

It was almost too much for her to take in all at once.

"Come, dear," said Louisa. "It's been a long day, and I think it's time for you to shed those dreadful trappings and discover the real you."

"The real me?" Poppy was confused.

Louisa neared her, turned her and casually began unfastening the laces of her gown. "The real you, Poppy. The woman who should not be confined by such atrocious garments..."

Poppy heaved a sigh of relief as the tight fabric eased around her breasts, but still raised a hand to catch the bodice. "I...I'm not sure...*here*?"

Louisa chuckled. "This room is my sanctuary, Poppy. No one enters without my express permission. Owen knows I have brought you here. We will be undisturbed."

Relaxing, Poppy allowed Louisa to strip off the ruffled gown, and stood in her chemise. "This is most odd, Louisa."

"And it will get odder still, my sweet." She pulled Poppy to the side of the bath. "I had my servants prepare this just for us.

Come on, I've added some of my favorite herbs. It's time for you to relax and enjoy yourself a little. I doubt you've had much chance, recently, have you?"

To her surprise, Poppy found herself stripped naked and reclining in sybaritic pleasure as scented water lapped at her body.

Must be that wine.

To her even greater surprise, she found herself talking. Sharing her innermost thoughts with Louisa, hiding nothing. She let her words fall freely, for one of the few times in her life, confident that for once she was talking to a woman who would understand.

Some thoughts were unbidden, yet they came out anyway. "I want to paint a male nude from life, Louisa. I am so...so...*bloody* frustrated when it comes to my models."

Louisa slipped her own gown off. "Go on."

"I've studied the human form. I've spent hours looking at techniques, learning about perspectives, colors, all that stuff. But I end up with a bowl of fruit or a vase of roses as a subject. You know, *suitable* things for women to paint. It's not *fair*."

"No. I agree. It's not fair."

Poppy had been so involved in her thoughts that she jumped as Louisa stepped into the other end of the large tub. Within moments, both women were submerged.

Louisa sighed contentedly. "Now this is much better."

Poppy shocked herself by agreeing. It *was* better. To share a moment like this with a woman who could *understand* was rare indeed.

As if by shedding their clothes, they had shed the barriers imposed on them by the society in which they lived. This was new territory for Poppy, and she was surprised to find how eagerly she embraced it.

She continued to expound on her theme. "The female body is no mystery to me, Louisa. I have sisters. I have a mirror. I know how to paint a nude woman."

She paused, thinking. "But a man? No. I've studied what I could of musculature, and men themselves, but all that silly padding obscures the form beneath. I have pictures in my mind, Louisa. Ones like...well, ones that are along the lines of..."

"Like the one you did of me and Owen?"

Poppy colored. "Yes."

"Pictures of a couple in the act of love?"

Poppy colored even more. "Yes."

"Any idea *why* you want to paint such pictures?"

Now *there* was a question few people had ever asked Poppy, and she idly swished her hand through the water as she considered it. Louisa passed her a soft cloth and some fragrant soap, and her mind was busy formulating her answer as she washed herself.

"Perhaps..." said Poppy slowly, "Perhaps because it...it shows the *honesty* of people."

"Go on." Louisa slipped lower into the water and rested her head on the back rim as her legs brushed Poppy's.

"Well...there are no *façades*. No coverings or trappings to hide behind. Nothing presented to another person other than what you are."

Poppy paused, struggling to find the right words. "It's a moment where everything is stripped away, leaving only the essence of a man and a woman. A time when they reveal so much more than just their bodies." She nodded. "*That's* what I want to capture. To show in a painting that the act of love takes place between more than the bodies of the lovers. It also takes place in the mind."

"Admirable. And so right too." Louisa grinned. "Let me ask you another question, now that you've answered the first one so eloquently. You say that the act of love reveals the pleasures of the mind. What do you know of the pleasures of the body?"

Poppy's mind blanked.

* * * * *

"She wants me to *what*?"

Damian's exclamation roiled around his glass of port and emerged as a squeak.

Owen grinned. "You heard me. Louisa wants you to pose for Poppy. Nude."

Damian gulped and swallowed a large mouthful of the pungent liquid. It burned as it went down, but not half as much as the idea of stripping naked for Poppy.

"Er...completely nude?"

"Completely nude."

"No clothes at all?"

Owen sighed. "I believe that is what the word 'nude' means, Damian. Yes. Totally naked. Starkers. In the buff. Nude."

Damian raised a hand. "All right. I get the point. I just wanted to make sure I'd heard you correctly."

He let the flush in his cheeks die down a little, and then glanced at Owen. "Why?"

Owen shrugged. "Who knows? The complexities of a woman's mind are way beyond me, Damian. I'm just a humble scientist. And when it comes to my wife...well, she constantly surprises me." He grinned again.

"I'll just bet she does," said Damian with feeling.

"Anyway, that's neither here nor there. The point is, Louisa sees something in this girl—I don't quite know what—but if there's one thing I've learned since our marriage, it's to trust Louisa's hunches."

Damian carefully put his glass down. "When?"

"Tomorrow."

To his confusion, Damian felt a pang of disappointment. He'd thought perhaps in the next hour would be good. So did his cock, which had begun to pay much closer attention to the direction this conversation was taking.

"Oh. Tomorrow. Well then…"

Owen was clearly struggling with laughter. "May I take it you're not averse to the idea?"

"Damn you, you sod. Of course not. I have no scruples when it comes to shucking off my breeches. I'm a Barbour, remember?" He grinned back. "What are they doing at the moment? Mixing paints?"

"No. They're in Louisa's private room."

Damian's eyes nearly crossed. He'd been honored once, long ago, with a glimpse into the amazing room and could vividly recall the dildoes, paddles, and other assorted sexual implements that were stacked around the walls.

Just imagining Poppy exploring them was heating his loins.

He shifted in his chair.

"Well …" Owen rose. "I'll tell Louisa that you're in favor of the idea."

Damian nodded.

"I may or may not see you in the morning. I have much to catch up on in my laboratory, and I doubt you'll want an audience for your…ahem…modeling assignment."

Damian glared at Owen. "I'm glad this is affording you some amusement, old chap."

Owen simply chuckled. "Time for bed, I think."

"Owen?"

Damian's words halted Owen's steps.

"Does Louisa expect me to fuck the girl, or what?"

Owen frowned a little. "I doubt that. Poppy is gently-bred, no matter what her inclinations are, artistically speaking." He stared at the fire. "But then again, as I mentioned earlier, Louisa's thoughts are often rather…rather *convoluted*, at times."

He raised his eyebrows helplessly at Damian. "I suppose you're going to have to follow your own instincts. Let's face it, putting a naked man in a room with an impressionable young girl…well, it *is* a set up for something to happen, isn't it?"

"Might I end up getting an arse full of buckshot and a forced march down some chapel aisle?"

"Oh, I doubt that Louisa would allow anything to go that far. She's too devious for that." Owen relaxed. "Trust her, Damian. She wouldn't have suggested this if she hadn't had her reasons. And I'm convinced that no matter how complex they may be, they're good ones. She has your interests at heart. And Poppy's too."

Damian sighed. That was a non-answer if ever he'd heard one.

He was still puzzling the matter over in his mind as he stripped for bed. To be naked in front of a woman would, as he'd told Owen, be no hardship. He had very little in the way of vanity, but knew he'd not be found wanting in the appearance department.

However, posing was a slightly different kettle of fish to fucking. Especially under those sharp grey eyes that would peer into every nook and cranny of his body.

His cock hardened at the thought, becoming fully erect and reminding him that there was more to Miss Poppy than her eyes.

Like those breasts. How he'd love to kneel astride her and squeeze them together, and then thrust his cock between them to that soft skin beneath her chin.

He began to ache, and without really thinking about it, his hand reached downwards. Lying back on the bed, Damian stroked his cock, his mind busy with images of a naked Poppy Adams, ringlets tousled, pleasuring him. She was probably a virgin, so his fantasies swerved from sinking into her cunt. He preferred not to be any girl's first lover. They were too unskilled and afraid, and, to put it bluntly, it made him nervous.

No, he dwelt on the other pleasant things they could do together.

He wondered if her thighs would be soft and white. If her mound would be thickly covered with that gleaming mahogany hair or downy with a slightly different shade.

Would her pussy gleam pink for him, or swell as red as the flower that bore her name?

How would she smell? And taste? *God damn.*

Damian groaned beneath his breath as the images plagued him. His hand was moving with purpose now, stroking in firm movements from the base of his cock to its head. A drop of his seed seeped from the tip, and he quickly smeared it over his hot flesh.

His thoughts blurred as his spine began that telltale tingle, alerting him that he was about to come.

His last thoughts before erupting were of Poppy's lips, full and wet, sinking onto his cock as he thrust into her mouth.

Damian Barbour found his release—alone, but with the picture of Poppy Adams firmly embedded in his brain.

Chapter 4

At the precise moment Damian Barbour was spilling his seed all over his belly, Poppy Adams was staring wide-eyed at Louisa across the bathwater.

"Pleasures of the body? I...I..."

"Just as I thought." Louisa reached into the water beside her and removed a slim glass wand. It had a rather distinctive shape.

"Do you know what this is?" Louisa held it aloft in the candlelight.

Poppy cleared her throat. "It's meant to be a man's...um...*thing*, right?"

"Cock, my dear. It's called a cock. Actually, it's called a variety of other things, depending on whom you ask. But for general purposes, the word cock does quite nicely."

"Yes. All right. If you say so."

"Here." Louisa stretched across the tub and handed it to Poppy. Who nearly dropped it.

"Oops...sorry. It's a bit slippery."

Louisa removed another one from the water. A *much* larger one. Poppy's eyes rounded once more. "Good lord." She dragged her gaze away from it to Louisa's amused face. "Do they come *that* big?"

"Sometimes." Louisa let her hands stroke the glass.

Poppy looked at the one she was holding, and tentatively imitated Louisa's movements.

"Poppy, do you know what a man's cock is for?"

"Of course. The man uses it to plant his seed in a woman and a child grows within her."

"Good." Louisa nodded practically. "You've got the basics, I see. But look at the shape and size of these two dildoes. Yes—" She intercepted a questioning look from Poppy. "That's what *these* are called. Dildoes. Pretend-cocks that women may use however they please, since they're not attached to a man." She paused. "Sometimes that can actually be a good thing."

Poppy was fascinated. Her hands had found the movement along the smooth surface of the...the...*dildo* to be quite natural, soothing almost. The glass was warm from submersion in the bathwater, and the effect was very pleasant.

She sighed in contentment and listened as Louisa continued her little lecture.

"Anyway, a man's cock must penetrate a woman to plant his seed. And a man's cock can be quite large. There are things that should happen to a woman's body first, before he comes inside her.""There are?"

"Oh yes. And very nice things they are too."

"Like what?" Poppy couldn't have held the question back if her life had depended on it. This was all so new, so exciting. So...so...arousing.

"A woman's body is full of areas that cause very pleasant responses when touched. Responses that will help her prepare to accept a man's cock."

"Oooh."

"For example..." Louisa's hand slipped beneath the water to her breasts. "A woman's nipples are full of exquisite sensations, Poppy. Have you never noticed?"

Poppy swallowed. "Not really. Mama always laced my bodices so tight, I barely felt my breasts, let alone anything else."

"Well, you are not laced now, are you?"

"No..."

"So put your hand on your belly, slide it up your skin and cup your breast."

Poppy hesitated.

"Go ahead. Cup your breast. Feel its weight in your hand. You're beneath the water, and it's not as if I'm going to be judging your breasts or your performance. This is for *your* pleasure, Poppy. I can take care of my own."

Slowly, Poppy did as she was bid. Her own skin seemed to have come alive beneath the sensual onslaught of Louisa's words and ideas, and when she reached the fullness of her own breast, something spurted into a lick of flame between her thighs.

Curiously she raised her eyes to Louisa.

"Good, Poppy. Now bring your thumb to your nipple and stroke it gently."

Poppy gasped. Her nipples were beading as she touched them, and the merest glance of her thumb sent shivers through her body and racing down to join that fire that was beginning to sparkle inside her.

"Louisa...I feel..."

"Strange?"

"Yesss," sighed Poppy.

"Experiment, love. Squeeze the nipple a little. Rub your dildo over the other breast at the same time. Find out what pleases *you*."

Louisa's voice was a little hoarse now, as she followed her own instructions beneath the water. Small waves lapped at the rim of the bath as both women explored their sensations.

Poppy dropped her head back slightly as she tightened her hold on her breast. A strong feeling of heat began to swamp her and she wanted to move. She didn't know how, but she spread her thighs instinctively.

"See how your body is preparing itself?" Louisa's murmur penetrated Poppy's brain. "Right at this moment, your cunny, that place where a man's cock will stroke into you, is moistening. Releasing a special liquid that will guide him and make his entrance easy."

"Really?" Poppy stared at the bathwater. "I don't see anything..."

"Touch between your legs, Poppy. Find out for yourself."

Poppy gulped, but her curiosity was now thoroughly aroused. And so, apparently, was the rest of her.

Slowly, she released her breast and slipped her hand down to the juncture of her thighs. As she brushed her mound, she jumped. "Oooh..."

Louisa smiled. "Yes, love. You've found a very important spot on your body. It's called a variety of things...your pearl of pleasure, nubbin, whatever...but it is properly known as your clitoris."

"Is that a Greek word?"

Louisa huffed out a laugh. "If you're thinking clearly enough to ask me that, you're not touching it correctly."

"Sorry." Poppy pondered the word for about thirty seconds—and then gently touched herself again. "Oh *God*."

Louisa smiled, and the water in her end of the bathtub began to ripple.

"Louisa..."

"Yes, sweetheart. It feels good, doesn't it?"

"Oh *my*." Poppy was entranced. Spirals of shivers spread over her skin as she gently stroked and explored herself. She slipped her fingers lower and encountered a different kind of moisture, hotter and more viscous than the bathwater. "Oh yes...I feel it...I'm getting wet..."

She glanced up at Louisa in excitement.

"This is what a man will do to you, love. He will touch you, tease you, bring your body to readiness with his hands, his mouth, and his cock..."

"His *mouth*?"

A sensual smile curved Louisa's lips. "Oh yes. Most definitely his mouth."

Poppy's head swam. Her nipples were tight now, and she could distinctly feel the water as it swirled around them, stirred by the movements of her hand between her legs.

"Poppy…take the dildo now…"

Poppy struggled to follow directions, blinking through her sensual haze.

"Put it between the lips of your pussy, darling. Just let it touch you. Rub yourself and your clit with it. Do what feels good. What feels right. Let your body tell you what it wants."

Blind to anything but her body's needs, Poppy obeyed.

The warm glass felt heavenly against her flesh, and she was surprised to find that she wanted *more* from this moment.

Carefully, she let the dildo slip between the folds of her body. It seemed to know where to go all by itself.

"Easy now. That's a very small dildo, but you *are* still a virgin."

Louisa's words of caution were lost on Poppy.

In fact, just about everything was lost on Poppy. The room faded, the bath blurred, and Louisa became just a presence far off in the distance. Poppy's whole world narrowed down to the place where a glass cock pressed into her secrets.

Her hand had found a certain spot that brought shivers of pleasure and arousal to her body, and now she was beginning to ache. A tremor passed over her as she daringly pressed the dildo deeper.

She could feel herself stretching, yearning, bathing the glass with moisture from her own body.

She needed—wanted more. Something was building within her that swept away her inhibitions and her fears. Her toes curled and her muscles tightened as she reveled in these new sensations.

Suddenly, the dildo slid deeper, as if pulled into her by her own desires.

She gasped aloud. "Oh God. *Louisa*...."

Louisa froze. "Are you all right? Poppy?"

Poppy couldn't hear her. There'd been a slight burning sting for a second or two, and then the cock had slipped inside her body, filling her cunny with hardness and pleasure.

It was...it was...*amazing*!

Her hand moved rapidly now, guided by some instinct she hadn't known she possessed. The fire had expanded to an inferno within her gut, and the feel of the glass inside her drove her into a frenzy.

She withdrew it fractionally and pushed it back again.

Her buttocks tightened, her mouth opened wide, and a shattering explosion drove the breath from her lungs on a scream.

Poppy came. In shuddering bursts of delight and physical pleasure, her world fell apart around her. Her cunt clamped down onto the glass in a rhythm that matched her pounding heart. She trembled and shook as her body rode out the waves of her orgasm, leaving her limp and astounded.

After long moments of shock, she gingerly withdrew the glass cock and refocused on Louisa. "Oh. My. God."

Louisa's face was a study in contrasts. Worry creased her brow, and yet her joy in Poppy's pleasure was clearly evident.

"My dear girl, are you all right?"

"I..." Poppy swallowed harshly. "I had no idea."

Louisa relaxed a little. "I had not intended for you to go so far, love. Are you hurt at all? Bleeding?"

Poppy tried to marshal her scrambled thoughts and looked around her, blinking at the bathwater she'd slopped over the side of the tub at her moment of orgasm. "I did make rather a mess..."

"Don't worry about that. It's you we need to concern ourselves with."

"I'm fine, Louisa." And Poppy realized she was. She was so relaxed she could have slept right there in the tub. Her muscles glowed, her heart had slowed to its normal rate, and she felt...fabulous.

"Thank God for that. Taking one's own virginity in a bathtub is not a common occurrence, you know."

"Is that what I did?" Poppy frowned. "I heard it was supposed to hurt dreadfully and one bled for days afterwards."

Louisa snorted. "Old wives tales. It's different for all women, of course, but if the conditions are right and your body is ready, then there should be no terrible discomfort."

"I did ride a lot as a child. Do you think that helped?"

"I doubt it. I dislike that excuse...'oh yes, I spent a lot of time on horseback. That's why it didn't hurt me to lose my virginity'. Too often that's used to cover an earlier indiscretion."

Louisa's lip curled in distaste. "Be that as it may, I'm just happy you're not in any pain." She rose from the tub, heedless of her nudity. "And the water is cooling. Time to dry off, I think."

She grabbed a nearby towel, and passed one to a rather limp Poppy. "Are you sure you're all right?"

Poppy grinned. "Oh yes. Most definitely."

She gathered her strength and stood on shaky legs, managing to climb out of the tub and into the towel Louisa held out for her. "A bit trembly, perhaps."

Louisa rubbed her briskly. "A natural occurrence. In the normal way of things, you'd be curled up against a sweaty chest right about now, and thinking of sleeping, not getting dressed."

Poppy considered that. "Is it different, Louisa? Different when there's a man...attached to the cock?"

Louisa chuckled. "Oh my, yes. The physical response is the same, but when you toss in the feelings of hard male flesh rubbing yours, lips suckling and kissing you all over, and sharing your orgasm with him...feeling him have his inside you...well, there are no words to describe it."

Amazingly, Poppy's body stirred at the images Louisa created. She must be a horribly wanton creature at heart.

"Thank you, Louisa."

"For what, dear?"

"For teaching me. For helping me not to be afraid of my body...of my...desires, I suppose you'd say."

Louisa hugged her. "These desires are part and parcel of being a woman, Poppy. I have always believed that women should be free to explore themselves. To discover their own sensuality. If men would only realize that it makes us better lovers in the long run, perhaps they'd be more supportive."

Poppy considered Louisa's words. "I think you're right. I don't know how many girls I've seen getting married without a clue as to any of *this*..." She waved her hand at the tub. "I owe you an enormous debt of gratitude."

They wrapped robes around themselves, and Louisa began to extinguish the candles that had gutted low around the room. "You can repay me by doing a splendid painting for this house, Poppy. One that shows your talent. And one that shows what you learned in here tonight...your passion."

Poppy's thoughts flew to Damian Barbour.

Oh yes. *Now* she could paint him.

The passion part...well, perhaps she'd find inspiration from her subject. Her breath caught at the possibility. Supposing she could see him naked? What would Damian's cock look like?

Up until tonight, Poppy would have blushed and hidden thoughts like that deep in the recesses of her mind. Now, to her astonishment, she found herself eagerly hoping that someday she might have the chance to find out.

Chapter 5

For the first time she could remember, Poppy was nervous as she busied herself with her paints.

Usually, she found the routine of preparing her supplies to be soothing, a ritual that flooded her with images, filled her mind with colors, and set her on the track to her own private heaven—the creation of her art on a canvas.

And the sumptuous room, filled with everything she needed, should have sent her into the dizzying heights of painterly bliss. It was very quiet, had light coming in at just the right angle, and there were several stretched canvases just waiting for her to bring her visions to life on them.

How Louisa had managed all this was beyond her. It had taken her breath away when she'd walked in.

"Like it?"

Louisa had asked the question, and Poppy's only reply had been a dropped jaw and a gasp. She was getting used to having the wind knocked out of her, apparently. It was the second time that morning it had happened.

The first was when she'd been awoken from the best sleep she'd had in ages to find a maid telling her that her bath was ready. *Two* baths in less than twenty-four hours. Her frugal family would have gone completely berserk.

She'd had her body scrubbed, her hair washed, and been dressed in a lightweight slip of a gown loaned by Louisa.

Her breasts were unconfined by tight laces, their fullness caressed by the soft blue fabric. And her *hair*. Thoroughly washed and dried by an attentive maid, Louisa had refused to allow her to crimp it, curl it or do anything with it. She'd just smoothed some fragrant lotion over it and brushed it to a shining mass, which now hung loosely down her spine.

She'd lost the capacity for speech when she caught sight of herself in the long mirror. She looked...she looked...pretty.

Louisa had simply smiled. "Don't worry about the gown. It's an old one, and will eliminate the need for us to explain any paint spatters on the one you wore yesterday. I want you to be free, Poppy. Free to paint as you will, what you will...let your feelings out onto the canvas."

Poppy had stared at her reflection. "Good God. I...I..."

"Come on. Your model will be along shortly."

It was that sentence that had stirred Poppy's brains into a tumble. "My *model*?"

Louisa calmly led her along a corridor and stopped in front of a door. "Yes. Didn't I mention it to you? Damian has agreed to pose for you. He will be your model today."

And it was *those* words that had turned Miss Poppy Adams from a dedicated artist into a trembling woman fiddling with her brushes.

Awash in a new self-awareness, Poppy dithered over her colors. She was going to paint Damian Barbour in the *nude*.. He was going to undress in front of her and display himself, every little bit of himself, for her eyes.

And, if she was very honest about it, for her pleasure too. It was going to be an amazing experience to have a live model, and she had a rather naughty feeling that she was going to enjoy every minute of it. She chewed her lip as she looked around the studio and pondered the best place to put him.

There was a long full drape of deep blue velvet tied against one wall, and with a quick move, Poppy shook it free. It fell into great swaths of color, puddling on the floor. Excellent.

Her artistic eye roamed the rest of the room. She focused on one small column, which probably had supported a vase or an urn of flowers at one time or another. Yes. That would do nicely.

She manhandled it over to the velvet drapery and positioned it half-in and half-out of the shadows. Umm…what else?

A large trunk revealed some theatrical props when Poppy curiously lifted the lid. Louisa had obviously cleared this room of some storage before converting it into a painter's studio. Poppy rummaged through the contents, emerging triumphantly with a painted wooden sword and a rather worn shield.

Excellent. An image was forming in her mind of the weary warrior she intended to paint. She had his weapons…now all she needed was *him*.

* * * * *

"He" at that very moment, was standing outside the studio door, indulging in a fit of rather unusual nerves. His shirt was open, his breeches scarcely tied tight enough to stay up, and he was barefoot. He was also wondering what the hell was the matter with him.

Perhaps it was the daylight. He wasn't used to the idea that he'd be getting naked inside that room, in the harsh light of day, in front of a woman who was going to look at him. *Really* look at him. He was used to being the one who did the looking.

He swallowed. Nothing ventured, nothing gained. He pushed the door open and stilled on the threshold, staring at Miss Poppy Adams.

Was it really *her*?

Gone were the ruffles and the tightly-laced abomination that had passed for her gown. And gone were the fashionably twisted curls that had hidden much of her face. Gone was the frumpy chit he'd met yesterday. In her place was…was…a glorious renaissance creature.

She seemed to stand taller, a straight sweep of rich mahogany hair falling like satin to the curves of her bottom. Parted in the center, she looked like a Madonna from some medieval work of art, and the simplicity of the gown added to the effect. Her breasts, unconfined by a bodice, rose softly against the fabric that flowed over them, and the full mounds moved freely beneath it.

God, she was lovely. He'd never have guessed such beauty was lurking beneath the trappings of yesterday. His cock stirred involuntarily as he watched her glide quietly around the room, moving things, stirring things, unaware of his presence. She was as lost in her tasks as he was in her appearance.

He mentally shook himself. Lord, what a pair they made. Or could make. He blinked away an erotic image of tangled limbs and hair like satin, and stepped inside.

"Good morning."

She jumped. So did her breasts. Oh fuck. He was in deep trouble here, and couldn't wait for more.

"Good morning, Mr. Barbour."

Her voice quavered slightly, and Damian relaxed. She was nervous too, and somehow, knowing that fact made this entire thing a whole lot easier on him.

"I think you could probably call me Damian, *Poppy*..." He kept his voice casual, but couldn't help letting a little warmth creep in as he used her name and saw a flicker of color pass across her cheeks. "Especially seeing as you'll be getting to know me quite...intimately."

The color became a definite blush.

She cleared her throat. "Yes, well, *Damian*... needless to say, I am very appreciative of your agreeing to Louisa's suggestion and posing for me this morning. I hope I'm not taking you away from anything important?"

She'd turned away and was busy now, slathering something on her canvas. Hiding. Not letting him see her face. He was not about to let her get away with it, and he strolled around the easel, watching her sure moves as she filled in a background wash of color.

"Not at all. This will be an interesting experience for me. I've never played the artist's model before. Not nude, anyway."

Poppy squelched a small sound that could have been a choke, a giggle or a sob. Whatever it was it made Damian's eyebrow lift slightly with subdued glee. Oh yes, this *was* going to be fun.

"So, shall I strip now?" He was pushing her a little. He wanted to watch her face as he revealed himself. Her expressive grey eyes would hide no secrets from him, he was sure of it.

She took a breath, making those delightful breasts tremble, and Damian realized that if she said yes, she was going to see some pretty fundamental male responses in action. He was already semi erect. He mentally shrugged. He was a man. She wanted to paint a man. She was going to see one doing what men did best. Getting aroused.

"That would be fine. I think, if you're willing, I'd like to have you stand by that pillar. You'll find a sword and shield there, and my thought is to portray you as a weary soldier, resting for a moment on the way home from the wars."

Damian began sliding his shirt from his shoulders. "Which wars?"

Her glance shot up to his face, and then down to his chest that was being revealed as the fabric slipped slowly away from his body. "Um, pardon?"

"Which wars? Which wars is he coming home from?"

She blinked. "Er...well..." She swallowed as he tossed his shirt away from him onto a nearby chair.

"The Peloponnesian wars?" His hands slid over his chest to his waist and he paused at the ties of his breeches.

"Uh..."

"The Persian wars?"

Poppy gulped as his fingers slowly drew the laces free.

"Come now, Poppy, you must have some notion. You have an idea in your mind, if I'm correct about how artists work? So this weary warrior...tell me more about him. Help me get an image of what you're looking for?"

"He's...he's..."

* * * * *

"Beautiful."

The word was out of Poppy's mouth before she could stop it. Damian had released the ties on his breeches and let them fall to the floor. She forgot things like wars, soldiers, classical Greek history, and her own name.

All she could do was look.

His body was a masterpiece. The morning light brushed his muscles with gold, and as he moved a little beneath her gaze his skin flowed like some kind of sinuous river over his personal landscape. Broad shoulders, touched with a little bronze, led downwards past a chest that looked strong enough to rein in the largest horse, but warm enough to lie against and drown in.

His waist dipped in slightly and beneath...Poppy caught her breath.

His skin was lighter, untouched by the sun, but sandy golden curls glowed between his legs and around his...his cock.

Like a magnet needle drawn to north, Poppy's eyes remained riveted on his male flesh. It moved as she stared, lengthening a little. She barely noticed the firm thighs, shapely calves or his feet, she was held captive by his...his...maleness...free and exposed to her gaze.

Oh God.

She gulped, torn between the urge to run and hide somewhere for a year or two or rush over to Damian and beg him to let her play with him. To beg him to play with her. To experiment with what rested between his legs, and what was dampening between hers.

Poppy was seriously conflicted, and could only drag in a sigh of relief as Damian took pity on her and turned away towards the pillar.

Only it was, in many ways, worse.

Damian's bottom was sculpted from some erotic artist's dream of what a male backside should be. Firm mounds of flesh, muscles moving beneath as he strode to the draperies and leaned over to pick up the sword and shield. Unconsciously, she licked her lips.

A dull ache started low in her belly, and she could feel her nipples as they hardened and dragged against the soft silk of Louisa's borrowed gown. So this was what it was like to be aroused...by a man. It was almost a pain, and so much of a pleasure.

She forced herself to turn to her canvas, confused and muddled by the thoughts that were flashing through her mind. Thoughts she probably shouldn't be having, but ones that flatly refused to go away.

Damian rose and thankfully held the shield before himself as he assumed an indolent pose against the column.

"So. Something like this?"

Poppy swallowed. "Um...yes. I think."

A small smile flashed over his lips and was gone so quickly that for a moment she wondered if she'd imagined it. "If you'd lean against the column a bit more, and perhaps cross your legs at the ankles?"

She gnawed on the inside of her lip, fighting a dozen urges she had yet to comprehend, and tried to focus on her art. Her art, not his cock.

"Now, let the sword dangle from your fingertips a little, if you would...remember, you're a weary soldier who's seen too much of battle..." She dragged her thoughts to the canvas before her. "Yes, that's right. Perfect."

And oh God he was.

Now that he'd all but hidden his luscious loins, Poppy's mind cleared enough to begin her painting in earnest. The vague background gave way to quick charcoal strokes of Damian's body, sagging against the column, as she outlined the figure in the pose she'd envisioned.

He was, as she'd so accurately said, perfect.

He'd slumped a little, letting his shoulders droop, and the shield and sword were held in a casual grip, as if the arms holding them were tired. His hair was mussed, his face settled into a blank look, which she imagined would be appropriate for an exhausted soldier, and he was the ideal model.

Losing herself in her work, Poppy's brushes flew frantically, capturing each line, each shadow, bringing to life the vision in her mind and the image before her, and marrying them into her painting.

She had no idea how much time had passed when Damian finally spoke.

"Will it disturb you if I talk?"

"What?" Her head jerked up and her eyes re-focused. On Damian. On the deliciously naked Damian. She smeared a stroke of purple on one of his thighs, and cursed quietly.

"Yes, I see that it will." His voice was light and amused, and she was almost surprised to hear it coming from what she now regarded as her weary warrior.

"No…no…please, go ahead. Maybe we should take a break for a few minutes. You must be getting tired…"

"I will admit that a stretch would feel good right about now. Are you sure it's all right?"

Poppy dipped her brushes in a nearby pot of turpentine oil. "Yes, absolutely. Please relax. I have the basics down, I believe."

So did he.

Damian sighed and stretched, letting the shield and sword clatter to the floor. Unabashed, he rotated his shoulders and flexed his knees.

Poppy gulped.

He strolled towards her, apparently unconscious of the delightfully complimentary rhythm thumped out by his cock against his legs as he walked. Poppy could have sworn she heard the thud of flesh against flesh. She closed her eyes for a moment or two, battling the heat that flooded her.

"Oh my, Poppy. Very nice. Very nice indeed."

His voice sounded from behind her, and she opened her eyes, knowing he was staring over her shoulder at what she'd painted.

"You have a lot of talent. Did you realize that?"

His voice was sincere, and she glowed from the compliment. She also glowed from the nearness of that naked body. He raised one hand and rested it on her shoulder, idly brushing her hair away so that he could touch her skin.

And that spot of skin burst into flames.

"I like the way you've blended the colors...right here..." Damian leaned in to point to a certain area, and slid his body against hers.

Poppy shivered at his touch.

"I very much admire your brush technique, too...right here..." He pointed to a spot on the far side of the canvas, and let his arm graze her breasts as he moved.

Poppy fought a fierce battle with a raging internal inferno.

"And I especially like..." His arm dragged back, catching her nipples and abrading them to the point of screaming pleasure. "I especially like...you."

Poppy surrendered.

His scent, his nearness, her bubbling excitement from her painting and the model for it, all contributed to her downfall and the quite dreadful thing she did next.

She stared at Damian.

Then she grabbed him by the shoulders and kissed him.

Chapter 6

All of Damian's seduction schemes vanished into thin air at the first touch of her lips. With innocent enthusiasm, she pressed them against his, and his arms slid around her, enfolding her against his nakedness with reflexive skill.

Her scent blended with the aromas of the oil paints and for a dizzying moment his head spun. She squirmed down his length, and the thin silk between them warmed and all but disappeared.

Damn. She had not a stitch on underneath.

He drew back a little and ran his tongue along her lips. "Open your mouth a little, Poppy," he whispered.

Her eyelashes flickered over the hot grey depths, and she obeyed. He pulled her close again, plunging his tongue into her mouth with all the enthusiasm of a starving man at the Prince Regent's banquet table.

He swallowed her gasp of surprise and let his movements teach her, encourage her, inspire her to mimic them.

She was a fast learner.

Yielding softly to his hands, her body melted against his, and she relaxed into his kiss, letting her instincts guide her now. And God, she had good instincts. There was a banked fire of passion inside this woman.

Damian's cock swelled with the longing to release it and bathe in its flames.

"This isn't fair." He breathed the words against her lips.

"What..." She opened her eyes and stared at him, the heat from her gaze taking his breath away.

"You're dressed. I'm not."

She probably didn't even realize she was rubbing herself against him. Damian did. With unerring accuracy his hand slid up her spine and tugged on the ties that secured the gown.

It fell to the floor at Poppy's feet as she gasped, swallowed, and pressed herself back against him, as if in a frenzy of eagerness to experience everything she could in thirty seconds.

"There's time, love. We have all the time in the world." *Right. I should tell my cock that.*

He swept one arm down behind her knees and picked her up in his arms. She was so hot against him, eyes wide with surprise, and he could smell her body's arousal mixed with the fresh flower scent of her skin.

In a few moments, he had her where he wanted her, beneath him, on the long couch that was tucked into a quiet corner of the studio.

He eased her hair out from beneath her spine and brushed the satin tresses away from her face. "Mmm. Better."

"Oh yessss," she breathed. "Damian, this is…this is…" She wriggled a little, making him suck in a quick breath. "*Splendid.*"

Damian smiled and returned to her lips, letting his hand stroke her skin as he settled himself half on her, half on the couch. The feel of her lush curves, her scent, her evident pleasure in every single thing he did, swelled his cock and touched something inside him. He found himself determined to give Miss Poppy every bit of pleasure he could provide, and maybe invent some more.

She sighed as he drew his mouth from hers, only to tense as he ran his lips over her neck and nipped lightly at the soft flesh.

"*Damian…*" His name was a breathy sigh, and his cock achieved unheard of proportions at the sound.

He could never remember hearing it whispered with such…passion. Or such desire. He slid lower, and gently circled her nipple with his tongue.

It beaded up rock hard, and delicately he lapped it, loving the moans and sighs each move brought from Poppy's throat.

He took it into his mouth and suckled.

Poppy cried out and grasped his head, threading her fingers through his hair and pressing him close. His eyes began to water as great tufts were tugged through her strong fingers.

The thought flashed through his mind that he'd be quite bald if he didn't do something quickly. He did something. He kept his mouth tight around her swollen breast and slid a hand down over her belly to the soft hair and the treasure it hid.

He found what he was looking for. Moisture was soaking her pussy, and he slipped his fingers through it, teasing, exploring and finally stroking the hard bud that her folds revealed.

Her hands fell away from his head, and he drew in a breath, releasing her nipple and moving to the other one, treating it to the same soft sucking and loving. Her legs were moving now, parting, twitching, allowing him freedom to touch all her secrets.

There was no hesitation in her moves. She might be an innocent, but she had clearly come to terms with her own needs and desires. And right now she desired him.

His feelings on the matter were not in doubt.

Every nerve ending in his skin was alive, energized, registering the slightest twitch of the woman beneath him. His heart pounded, his head filled with the scent of her and the textures his fingers were discovering, and his cock…well, there were no words.

He ached, painfully and lustfully, to sink deep into the boiling silk he knew was waiting for him.

But for once in his life, something held him back. Not her virginity, nor her innocence, but something *else*. Something that whispered to him that taking Poppy would change the dynamics of his life. That after her, nothing would ever be the same again.

Her passion rose beneath his skilled fingers, and her honey coated his skin with warmth.

He pulled away from her, staring at her, loving the flush that had covered her skin, the way her nipples were taut and shiny from his mouth and the fact that her legs were shamelessly parted for his touch.

Her eyes slowly opened, dilated with need. They looked straight into his.

And went beyond. Deep into Damian's soul.

Dear God. What was happening to him? "I'm going too fast…" It was more an admonition to himself than to Poppy, but she heard him.

"No, Damian…no you're not. I want this. I want *you*. I want to know all of it…teach me."

Her gaze never faltered. Her desire had been fully and totally aroused, and she *wanted*. She wanted *him*.

The thought that she might ever want someone else like this darted through his mind like a savage bolt. No. Absolutely not. Never. He would be her first. And her *only*.

He grabbed onto his control with his teeth clenched, and reached past the arm of the couch to where some of her brushes lay ready. He grasped the softest one he could find.

"Poppy," he whispered. "My turn."

She licked her lips. "For what?"

He smiled. Ignoring his cock, his desperate need to come, and the dizzying sight of such wonderful nakedness sprawled in his arms, Damian focused on the task he'd just assigned himself.

"I'm going to paint *you*."

* * * * *

"I…what?"

Poppy's mind struggled to comprehend what Damian was talking about. And failed. She couldn't think, couldn't organize words into sentences, could barely remember her own name.

The world, for Poppy Adams, had narrowed down to Damian's body and the absolutely incredible things he was doing to hers. She bit back a cry of distress as he moved away from her.

"Shhh...love...I'm still here..." His murmur reassured her, but she was still puzzled. Shouldn't he have claimed her by now? She knew her body was ready, *more* than ready. Her experiences under Louisa's tutelage had awakened her knowledge of all things sensual, and Damian was advancing her lessons into realms that surpassed even her wildest fantasies.

But he'd stopped, or paused, anyway.

Then she felt it. The lightest touch of her paintbrush across her pussy. It swirled and she couldn't hold back the moan as he ran the soft bristles through her own liquids.

"Close your eyes, Poppy. I want you to *feel*..."

Was he mad? She was feeling so much right at this moment that if she didn't feel something else, something long and hot and hard, very shortly, she was going to have another one of those explosive moments all by herself.

Poppy bit down on her response and waited. And then...there it was.

She gasped. The wet brush was circling her breasts, the merest flicker registering on her sensitized skin like flames. He was, in the truest sense of the word, *painting* her.

The circles diminished in size until he was ringing her nipple. The bristles were soft and moist, but the touch sent her skyrocketing into bliss. She moaned.

"Oh God, Damian..."

And when his tongue followed the path of the brush, licking and sucking her own moisture from her skin, she cried out with the pleasure of it.

"I know, love," he soothed. The brush disappeared, only to reappear at her pussy, swirling, tickling, dipping once more into the honey-pot that was bubbling over with enthusiasm and desire.

The other breast received the same treatment.

She was going to die. Poppy became convinced that it would be impossible to withstand so much pleasure and survive it. Her moans became groans as his mouth suckled and laved and licked once more.

But apparently, death was not imminent. Just more pleasure.

His artistic adventure took him to her navel, and he ringed that with a firmer touch, nipping this time with his teeth, soft love bites that were followed by a smooth stroke of his tongue.

She was losing her mind. Perhaps it was insanity that would result from the act of loving, not death. Her flesh burned and shivered according to his touch. He was blending the sensations within her as skillfully as she blended her colors. He was her artist, she was his canvas. And together?

They were a masterpiece of impossibly sensual dimensions.

Just when she thought she could catch her breath, his touch came again. This time he left the brush where it was. Swirling and teasing its way through the swollen folds of the flesh between her thighs. She cursed the back of the couch for being there and preventing her from opening herself even more, and her muscles trembled with the need to spread her legs for him. For Damian.

He slid off the cushions onto the floor and with a sigh of pleasure Poppy opened her thighs wide, wantonly inviting him into her secrets.

Damian accepted her invitation.

The brush teased her folds and found her clit, tickling and caressing it with slow, agonizingly slow strokes, until she was sweating, moaning and writhing into its touch.

It stopped.

Poppy held her breath.

And then he touched her with his mouth. He slid between her legs, parting them as far as they would go with his wide shoulders. The shock of feeling his nakedness against her thighs was quickly overwhelmed by the shock of feeling his tongue against her...*there*.

Wet and heated, it probed and licked and teased her, driving her up to amazing new heights and making her sob with the pleasure of it.

"Oh *God*..." The words were forced from her throat as her whole body began to shudder at his touch. His hands were gripping her thighs hard, and the sensation simply added to the whirlwind she found herself riding.

His tongue grew more demanding, thrusting now, into that place that was weeping for his touch.

She shouted out loud, heedless of where she was, aware only of the relentless pressure driving her insane.

How much more could her body take?

He was lapping at her, like a cat, licking the cream and spreading it around, delving into each and every tingling fold and throbbing depth.

"Damian..." It was a strangled scream, muted to a whisper by the desire clogging her throat.

"Poppy..." Damian rasped her name, as hoarse as she. "I want to take you. But I don't want to hurt you..."

He raised himself up on his elbows and moved, letting his cock continue the teasing movements that his tongue had started.

She opened her eyes weakly and stared at him. So handsome, face flushed and gleaming with her own juices. His blue eyes were blazing at her, and she struggled with the notion that he was asking her something.

Christ in heaven. She was toppling into a pit of sensual madness and he was asking her something.

His cock was searing her pussy, nuzzling between the lips of her cunt of its own accord.

"I don't want to hurt you, Poppy."

His words finally percolated through her mental fog. "Hurt me?"

Damian nodded and bared his teeth as his cock nudged her open even more. The muscles in his neck were taut, and his body straining.

"You'll only hurt me if you stop, damn it..." She bit the words out, panting as the head of his cock brushed against her clit.

He hesitated.

Poppy damn near screamed. If *he* wouldn't, then....

She raised her legs, clasping him between her thighs. With instincts she never knew she possessed, Poppy moved her ankles behind him to his spine and held him close. Closer...

He was breaching her, sliding around in the ocean of wetness his loving had brought from her, and she had never, *ever*, wanted anything so much in her whole life.

She'd die if he stopped now.

She'd kill him too. Right before she died.

"Do it Damian. Please. Dear God, *do* it..."

And to make sure Damian Barbour fully understood the level of her needs and her desires, Miss Poppy Adams locked her ankles, moved her hips and thrust upwards, pulling him down towards her at the same moment.

His cock slid into her body, and she came.

* * * * *

A split second of terror that he'd hurt her was followed by the most cataclysmic orgasm Damian could ever remember having. He exploded inside Poppy like some mythical fountain, one that refused to cease its endless cascade.

She was hot, tight, and her orgasm was shaking her to the core. It was shaking him to the core too. He'd slipped inside her with no checks or fumbles to bar his way, and she was now clinging to his body, his cock, and his soul.

All three were in a state of near madness.

As was she. Her cries rang in his ears, her skin was wet with sweat and her own juices, and her body shuddered with spasms of bliss as she welcomed him, sharing every little bit of her orgasm with him.

She held nothing back. Every shiver and shake, every panting gasp, it was all there, beneath him, in his arms. She rode her crest with pleasure and joy and he hung on for dear life, matching her ecstasy with his own.

He wanted to watch, to see her as she came, but he was helpless before the onslaught of his own responses. He pumped himself into her, his balls in a knot, his heart in his throat, and every muscle in his body straining with the need to lose himself in her.

Dear God. It was...beyond everything.

Finally, after what seemed like uncounted eons of bliss, the shudders subsided and the moment was over. Damian's cock softened at last, lying snugly in the warm liquids within Poppy's cunt.

He didn't want to move. He didn't want to withdraw. He just wanted to lie here, nestled inside her. Forever.

And the fear began.

Chapter 7

God fucking *damn!*

He'd done everything *right.*

He'd held Poppy close in his arms, soothing her skin with loving strokes, caressing her down to earth and letting her regain her senses.

Then he'd let her talk, and for once had actually listened, as she tried to tell him how he'd made her feel.

How her world had turned upside down, inside out, and had some kind of internal cataclysm while doing it. He'd watched her expressive face as she tried to explain the inexplicable, and smiled through her futile efforts.

He knew.

His world had done precisely the same thing. And it had done it all over again when she'd snuggled her head onto his chest, tangled her legs with his, and gently slipped off to sleep.

He'd lain, motionless, holding her to his heart, listening to her breathe and wondering what had happened to him.

He'd ignored the chills that had crept over him, and the insistent voice telling him things he didn't want to hear.

Things like...if he released her now, he'd be the biggest fool in Christendom. Things like she had knocked his world askew, and was the only one who would ever be able to put it right.

Things like...like there would never be another Poppy. Another moment like this.

He'd ignored all those thoughts, and gently eased himself from the couch, covering the sleeping woman with a soft blanket. He needed to think, needed some time alone to sort out what had just happened. And where he was going from here.

He'd emerged from the studio, tumbled in appearance and troubled in mind, only to find a note awaiting him from Nick. He had been summoned to London. On a matter of some urgency.

Which explained why his thoughts were accompanied by the pounding of his horse's hooves along the road, but didn't explain why he felt an odd hurt, an ache around his heart.

Nor did it explain the almost overwhelming urge to turn around, head back to Montvale, and find Poppy, and…and…

His horse stumbled slightly, and Damian grabbed a tighter hold on the reins.

Fuck. What the hell was the matter with him?

* * * * *

Poppy stared out of the window in the studio, watching the rain pelt down through the trees and drip onto the green lawns below. She empathized. She too, felt grey and cloudy, and with a tendency to burst into rain at the slightest thing.

It had been five long days since she'd lain with Damian. Five days of reliving the most incredible experience of her life. Every single second of it. She'd gone to bed unfulfilled and alone, and tossed sleeplessly through most of her nights at Montvale, because as soon as she dropped off, she dreamed of him. All over again.

Louisa had looked distressed as she brought the news to Poppy that Damian had been called to London.

Poppy had done her best to deal with the blow. She hadn't curled up into a sodden and whimpering ball of tears, although the inclination had been strong. She hadn't spent her time mooning about the house, pining for a lover long gone.

No, she hadn't done any of these things.

She'd painted.

Wisely, Louisa had left her alone with her canvases and her brushes, perhaps guessing that only in the company of such familiar friends could Poppy come to terms with her experiences and the new colors that life had painted into her brain.

Four completed paintings stood drying on one side of the room. One for each day he'd been gone.

And the subject matter was always the same. Damian Barbour.

The first was the warrior she'd begun on that fateful morning. The second, a more casual pose, in his dark evening garments, smiling across a dinner table.

The third had him on a wide hillside, staring out at nothing in particular, and the fourth, asleep on a riverbank.

It was the fifth painting that occupied her this morning. And a need to recapture the exact moment that had driven her to the window and the grey skies beyond.

Sighing, she returned to her work and picked up her brushes and her palette.

A little shiver ran through her as she stared at the image taking shape on the canvas.

It was Damian. Of course.

But it was the moment when he'd reared up over her, taking his weight on his hands and staring down at her with the fire of a thousand suns burning in his eyes. The moment when his cock had found her pussy and started the short journey to her heart and her soul.

It was a moment forever branded into Poppy's brain, and she hoped that by painting it, she could exorcise it from her consciousness.

She worked harder, shadowing the muscles as they rippled in his forearms, and highlighting the cords in his neck that had showed his control. She blinked as her brush captured the tousled head of hair that had flown every which way with each of his thrusts, and she bit back a sob as she tried to capture the expression that lit his blue eyes.

She painted like a madwoman now, frantic to capture the moment forever, to wrench it from her heart and transfer it to the canvas. Her brushes flew, paint spattered everywhere, and Poppy ignored it all.

This wasn't her mind, her techniques or her experience doing the painting. This was her soul.

Tears fell from her eyes and she didn't even notice them. Her nose ran and she sniffed and crossly wiped it on a paint-smeared bit of cloth. A servant respectfully left a tea tray for her. She barely heard him.

She was a woman possessed. By the image of a man she'd never have. A man whose eyes were now staring out at her from the painting, making her hot all over again.

She shivered, wondering if a window was open somewhere. Or maybe it was just the vision she'd painted. She closed her eyes, and let herself remember.

Remember the strength of the arms that had surrounded her, the touch of the lips on her neck, and the heat of the body that had aroused hers to such incredible peaks of pleasure.

She could almost feel it. Her nipples hardened. She could almost smell his special scent.

Almost feel the arms creeping around her body, cupping her breasts...breathing on her neck...

"I love you, Poppy."

She almost heard his voice. Saying what she desperately wanted to hear.

"I said...I love you, Poppy."

Brushes flew, oils spilled, and Poppy jumped a foot in the air, only to be caught and swung around against a hard chest.

Damian smiled down at her, blue eyes blazing, wet strands of hair lashed across his cheeks, and held her close.

Her mouth opened, but no sound came out. Her throat, her brain, her entire being was simply frozen.

Until he kissed her.

Dampness from the rain met her fingers as she clawed at his shoulders, but she didn't care.

It was really *Damian*. He was really *here*. He was really *kissing her*.

Her mental functions began sorting themselves out, and she dragged her lips from his.

"*What* did you say?"

His laugh blew away the last of her doubts. "I said, and pay close attention please, because I've never said this to another woman—*ever*—" He tightened his hold on her. "I love you. It took me about two days without you to realize it, but I do. I love you."

"Well, *hell*." Poppy's lungs expanded with joy. "Two days? It took me five minutes. And, just so that we're both clear on this, I love you too." She raised a hand to his cheek and touched him, loving the roughness beneath her palm. "I don't think I could ever say it to anyone else. *Ever*."

"Not even our children?"

Once again the breath left Poppy's lungs.

Damian took advantage of her shock, kissed her again soundly and, swooping her up in his arms, strode from the studio and down to the parlor where Owen and Louisa were waiting.

"I...but...you...*Damian*..."

Louisa laughed. "I see you have the Barbour touch when it comes to rendering a woman speechless, Damian."

Damian set his burden down with a grin. "Nick's not the only one with charm in the family."

"I...I..." Poppy cursed beneath her breath. Perhaps at some point over the next month or so she'd get a coherent word out of her mouth.

"Come, love. Sit. Let me tell you about my hurried trip to London."

She found herself tugged onto the couch, plied with tea and biscuits, cuddled close to Damian, and engaged to be married, all within the space of ten minutes. She'd also had a spot of paint removed tenderly from her nose.

"...So when the post in Brussels opened up, Nick immediately thought of me. I had to get back and shake hands with the right people, and it was a *fait accompli*. Behold..." He spread his arms. "You see before you the new Aide to His Majesty's Ambassador to Belgium."

Poppy gulped. "Really?"

Damian grinned. "Oh, and his future wife, of course."

Poppy choked. "*Really?*"

"You're repeating yourself, love." Damian's smile swept the room. "I have the license, I have your father's permission..."

Poppy blinked. "*Really?*"

Damian dropped a kiss on her nose. "Yes, REALLY." He smiled tenderly at her. "Your parents were a bit hesitant at first, but a few words with your father straightened everything out."

"*Real*...um...my goodness."

"It seems that anyone who is a cousin of the mighty Lord Barbour is considered acceptable. You have your family's permission to marry me, sweetheart."

Poppy snorted. "As if I needed it. I'd marry you with or without anyone's permission."

Damian's eyes turned hot. "Good."

"So then, off to Brussels?" Owen's voice eased the vibrating tension that had sprung up between them when Damian's gaze had brushed Poppy's face.

Damian answered. "Yes. As soon as possible. I'm hoping my wife can find plenty to paint over there, not to mention all those museums filled with the Flemish artists..."

Poppy's eyes began to sparkle.

"And you, Damian…my *husband*…" The word came out as the promise of a future to be lived to the fullest, and Damian's hand pulled Poppy even closer to his heart.

"What will you be doing in Brussels?"

The room disappeared around Poppy as Damian's blue gaze met her own with such passion in it that her breath caught in her throat.

"Me?" His voice was low and his lips neared hers. "I'll be doing what I was born to do. I'll be pleasuring Miss Poppy."

* * * * *

"Well, that came off rather well."

Owen turned Louisa from the large front steps of Montvale House and led her back inside. They'd waved farewell to the happy couple, and the carriage had rolled off towards a honeymoon, London and a ship to Brussels.

They were alone at last.

"It certainly did." She grinned up at him, loving just to look at this man who had held her heart for the past five years.

"So how did you know they'd make a match of it?" Owen busied himself with decanters, pouring a little of the brandy they both loved into glasses.

"I didn't."

Owen blinked. "You didn't? But you put Damian, naked, in the same room with an impressionable young miss…Good Lord, Louisa…that was risky. Supposing it hadn't worked out?"

"Then she'd have stabbed him with a paintbrush or given him another knee in the balls." Louisa's voice was calm, and Owen laughed.

"You were *that* sure of Poppy, then?"

"After our session in my room, yes. She was a bundle of creative and passionate talent, yearning to become a woman. She has a brave and adventurous spirit, Owen…I knew she'd come to no harm. And perhaps find something…special…with Damian. He's not unlike her in many ways."

Owen shook his head. "I'll never understand women."

Louisa allowed a sensual smile to curve her lips, and ran her tongue suggestively along the rim of her glass. "Perhaps it's time for another lesson in your education, my love."

Owen tugged at his cravat. "Hmm…Very well. I'm always in favor of…education."

"Good." She tipped her head and looked at him. "I think I'm in the mood for something *spicy* this evening."

Owen's eyes opened wide and a bulge appeared beneath his breeches. He swallowed. "Me too."

And if the Montvale House cook wondered about the ginger root missing from her pantry the following morning, she never said a word.

THE END

About the author:

Born and raised in England not far from Jane Austen's home, reading historical romances came naturally to Ms. Kelly, followed by writing them under the name of Sarah Fairchilde. Previously published by Zebra/Kensington, Ms. Kelly found a new love—romanticas! Happily married for almost twenty years, Sahara is thrilled to be part of the Ellora's Cave family of talented writers. She notes that her husband and teenage son are a bit stunned at her latest endeavor, but are learning to co-exist with the rather unusual assortment of reference books and sites!

Sahara Kelly welcomes mail from readers. You can write to her c/o Ellora's Cave Publishing at 1337 Commerce Drive, Suite 13, Stow OH 44224.

Also by SAHARA KELLY:

- Alana's Magic Lamp
- Finding the Zero-G Spot
- The Glass Stripper
- Hansell and Gretty
- A Kink In Her Tails
- Madam Charlie
- Persephone's Wings
- Peta and the Wolf
- Sizzle
- The Sun God's Woman
- Mesmerized – with Ashleigh Raine & Jaci Burton
- Mystic Visions – with Myra Nour & Ann Jacobs

Why an electronic book?

We live in the Information Age—an exciting time in the history of human civilization in which technology rules supreme and continues to progress in leaps and bounds every minute of every hour of every day. For a multitude of reasons, more and more avid literary fans are opting to purchase e-books instead of paperbacks. The question to those not yet initiated to the world of electronic reading is simply: *why?*

1. *Price.* An electronic title at Ellora's Cave Publishing runs anywhere from 40-75% less than the cover price of the <u>exact same title</u> in paperback format. Why? Cold mathematics. It is less expensive to publish an e-book than it is to publish a paperback, so the savings are passed along to the consumer.

2. *Space.* Running out of room to house your paperback books? That is one worry you will never have with electronic novels. For a low one-time cost, you can purchase a handheld computer designed specifically for e-reading purposes. Many e-readers are larger than the average handheld, giving you plenty of screen room. Better yet, hundreds of titles can be stored within your new library—a single microchip. (Please note that Ellora's Cave does not endorse any specific brands. You can check our website at www.ellorascave.com for customer

recommendations we make available to new consumers.)

3. *Mobility.* Because your new library now consists of only a microchip, your entire cache of books can be taken with you wherever you go.

4. *Personal preferences are accounted for.* Are the words you are currently reading too small? Too large? Too...**ANNOYING**? Paperback books cannot be modified according to personal preferences, but e-books can.

5. *Innovation.* The way you read a book is not the only advancement the Information Age has gifted the literary community with. There is also the factor of what you can read. Ellora's Cave Publishing will be introducing a new line of interactive titles that are available in e-book format only.

6. *Instant gratification.* Is it the middle of the night and all the bookstores are closed? Are you tired of waiting days—sometimes weeks—for online and offline bookstores to ship the novels you bought? Ellora's Cave Publishing sells instantaneous downloads 24 hours a day, 7 days a week, 365 days a year. Our e-book delivery system is 100% automated, meaning your order is filled as soon as you pay for it.

Those are a few of the top reasons why electronic novels are displacing paperbacks for many an avid reader. As always, Ellora's Cave Publishing welcomes your questions and comments. We invite you to email us at service@ellorascave.com or write to us directly at: 1337 Commerce Drive, Suite 13, Stow OH 44224.

Printed in the United States
22744LVS00006B/1-72

Inside Lady Miranda

Lord Nicholas Barbour has entered a very strange wager in the Betting Book at White's. It's going to take an unusual woman to win the bet—one who is desperate, clever, and has nothing to lose. A woman like Lady Miranda...

Miss Beatrice's Bottom

Harry Boyd, Earl of Dunsmere, is a Corinthian, Rake and highly regarded lover, known for his hot lust rather than his warm heart. Rescuing a damsel in distress is quite out of character for the earl. But then again, Harry is about to learn that nothing is ordinary about Miss Beatrice...

Lying With Louisa

The scientist and the sensualist. Louisa Cellini's sensuality is boundless, as is Professor Owen Lloyd-Jones' intellectual curiosity. When an explosive twist of fate brings them together they learn that the answers to some questions involve more than the mind and the body - they also involve the heart.

Pleasuring Miss Poppy

Miss Poppy Adams' passion is her oil painting. Damian Barbour, a handsome London rake, is her model. Their desires blend like the colors on a palette, and with a little help from Louisa and her toys, Damian finds his goal in life...pleasuring Miss Poppy.

10.99 USD   7.99 GBP

ISBN 1-4199-5000-2

51099

9 781419 950001

ELLORA'S CAVE
ROMANTICA PUBLISHING

Purchase this e-book and others @
WWW.ELLORASCAVE.COM